LACY

LACY

Ilyon Chronicles – Book Five Novella

Jaye L. Knight

INK
DRAGON
PRESS

Lacy
Ilyon Chronicles – Book Five Novella
Copyright © 2018 by Jaye L. Knight
www.ilyonchronicles.com

Published by Ink Dragon Press

Ilyon Map © 2023 by Jaye L. Knight

Ilyon

Samara

Amberin
Stonehelm

Sinnai Mts.

Graylin Valley

Arcacia

Sidian
Ocean

Dunlow
Fort Rhall
Kinnim

Valere
Landale

Ardakin Bay
Mernin
Keaton

Fort River

Arda

Falspar
Troas

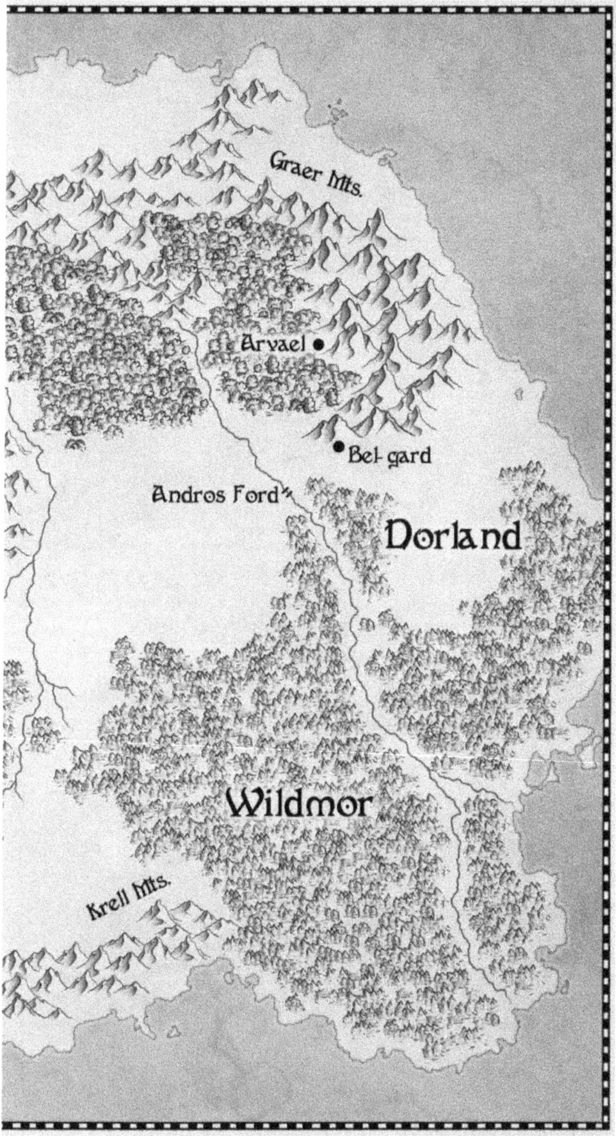
Graer Mts.
Arvael
Bel-gard
Andros Ford
Dorland
Wildmor
Krell Mts.

AARON STEPPED OUT of the narrow townhouse he shared with Timothy and four other single men from their congregation. It wasn't much, but it had so far kept them warm and sheltered from the brutal winter. In fact, it was better than the cottage they used to have in Dunlow. At least the construction was more solid. He glanced up the street and then to the sky. Clouds blocked the evening sun, but it hadn't snowed in almost a week—a record for this winter. Elôm willing, the worst of the harsh weather was finally behind them.

Footsteps scraped the icy cobblestone to his right as Timothy joined him. "Are you coming to the warehouse?"

He looked over at his younger brother. Most of the congregation would gather tonight to hear Timothy share the message he'd worked on for the last couple of days.

"I'll meet you there later. I'm going to stop at the Briar first."

Timothy responded with only a brief nod. Some might have questioned Aaron's frequent visits to the tavern, but Timothy understood.

1

Aaron waited until the other men joined Timothy before he turned in the opposite direction. Numbers were the key to safety in Valcré, and he always felt better when Timothy didn't travel alone.

He strode purposefully toward the rougher district of the city. In his experience, confidence went a long way in deterring an attack. People were less likely to try to rob you if they knew you could handle yourself.

He passed very few people on the streets. Although spring was on its way, the icy breeze held no hint of it. It would have to warm up considerably before the majority of the population ventured outdoors for more than brief errands or pressing business. Those who did prowl in the shadows were likely up to no good. Aaron checked over his shoulder often to make sure no one followed.

Before long, he rounded a familiar corner into a narrow street and spotted the sign hanging above the door of the Briar Pub. He wouldn't have admitted it to anyone, but his pulse kicked up a notch.

A blast of warm air and voices hit him as he pushed the door open and stepped inside. The tavern's common room was filling up as it normally did this time of evening when laborers finished their daily shifts. He scanned the room, recognizing several men. He'd made a point of making connections in the city. One never knew when they might need assistance or information.

A couple of Alex Avery's men sat in the corner and offered him an inconspicuous nod. Ever since the ordeal with the remedy and helping to save Avery's life, Aaron had cultivated a relationship with the smuggling group. Avery had even offered him a position among his men. As lucrative as that might have been, Aaron turned it down. There were more honest ways to help people.

But they weren't what brought Aaron here. His gaze rested briefly on each of the barmaids making their rounds, but none of them bore the face he sought. He suppressed a sigh and stepped up to the bar. An older woman stood there, just as provocatively dressed as the younger barmaids. Tess often managed the bar while Victor, the barkeeper, visited with his patrons.

"Aaron," she said with a lively grin, "what can I get you?"

He leaned an elbow against the bar and glanced around the room again. "Ale."

She filled a mug and set it before him. As Aaron fished a coin from his pocket, she leaned over the bar and whispered as if sharing a secret.

"She should be down in a few minutes." The woman winked at him, her heavily painted eyelids a deep violet.

"Thanks." He grabbed his ale and walked over to an empty table near the roaring fireplace. He took off his coat and draped it over the back of his chair before sitting down. Victor eyed him from across the room, but as long as Aaron bought an ale when he came, the man had no reason to complain.

Aaron sipped the brew and waited. He picked out bits and pieces of the conversations that buzzed around him, but he fixed his gaze on the steps leading to the rooms upstairs.

Several minutes later, a red skirt swished into view. The rest of the woman appeared, her dark hair falling in soft waves over her shoulders and her eyes glittering with candlelight. Aaron straightened, and a smile tugged at his lips. However, it died with the solid thump of boots that came behind her. A scruffy lout descended the stairs. Aaron bristled and cleared his throat, fighting the animosity building up inside him. No matter how many times he witnessed it, the scene always turned his stomach sour.

At that moment, Lacy's eyes caught with his. Her blank expression tensed, her eyes wide as she held his gaze.

The man behind her rested his grubby hand on her almost bare shoulder. She broke eye contact with Aaron and turned to the cad, who grinned leeringly. He tucked a coin down the front of her bodice and whispered something. Aaron tightened his fingers around his mug. Lacy smiled at the scoundrel, but the way it strained her face was painful. Aaron had to mentally force himself to remain in his chair. Causing a scene now wouldn't offer Lacy the help she needed.

Lacy then turned to the bar, clearly avoiding Aaron's gaze. He shifted his attention to her latest patron. The man traded a couple of lewd comments and hearty laughter with friends of his at a nearby table before ambling to the door. Aaron sent an icy look after him. The lout was probably married. Maybe even a father. If Aaron had just five minutes alone with him, he'd—

Light footsteps interrupted his darkly satisfying thoughts. Lacy approached his table, and he cleared his face of all hostility. She still struggled to maintain eye contact, but he smiled to put her at ease. In response, her own smile peeked out—soft and genuine, and not at all like the one she had given the other man.

"Aaron," she said softly, "can I get you anything?"

He slowly shook his head and tipped his nearly empty mug. "I've had enough." He stared up at her, and her lips twitched with another smile. "It's your night off, isn't it?"

"Yes. I just have to make one more round and then I can leave."

Aaron lifted up a silent prayer and spoke quietly. "There's a meeting tonight. Perhaps you'd like to come?"

Her chin dipped as she stared down at the table, discomfort again shadowing her expression. "You would invite me even after…" Her gaze darted to the stairs before meeting his again. So much torment hid behind her shining eyes.

"I'll always invite you if there's a chance you'll come." His fingers itched to reach for her hand, but he kept them firmly around his mug.

She released a long breath, and Aaron held his. But then she shook her head. "Not tonight. I need to be with my mother and sisters."

Aaron swallowed down the sting of another disappointment and smiled. "Well, you're always welcome."

A longing flickered in her eyes as if she desperately wanted to believe that.

"Thank you," she murmured and turned to go, but Aaron stopped her.

"Do you want me to walk you home? I can wait until you're finished. It's already getting dark out there." He didn't want to admit how much he had come to hate the idea of her walking to and from the tavern alone all this time. His mind was too good at serving up all the countless dangers a woman faced out there without an escort.

Again, she looked as if she wanted to accept but quickly said, "Thank you, but no. I'll be fine."

Aaron got the distinct feeling she was trying to maintain a certain distance from him.

"All right." He stood up and reached for his coat, giving her a smile to make sure she knew he wasn't upset. He stuck his arms into his sleeves and reached into his pocket. Withdrawing a large coin, he laid it on the table near her. "Just in case your family needs a little extra."

Lacy started to protest, but he held up his hand. "I insist."

He stepped around the table and walked toward the door.

"Thank you," her soft voice murmured after him.

He cast a smile over his shoulder and pulled open the door.

Icy dusk had fallen. He tugged on his gloves and strode toward the main street. Now that he was alone and back out in the cold, his disappointment set in once more. He just wanted to get Lacy out of this life. He could see in her eyes how much she hated it. If only she could have found another way to provide for her family after her father's death. Aaron knew well the desperation of protecting family in these circumstances. The two of them were quite similar really. How many times had Aaron nearly worked himself to death to provide for Timothy and Josan? Unfortunately, there weren't nearly as many moral opportunities for women in this city as there were for a hardworking man.

Aaron's senses sharpened in an instant. Two men skulked at a corner just ahead of him, casting shady glances in his direction. He brushed the edge of his coat away from his sword so he could grab it quickly if the need arose. It would also send a clear message to the men that he wouldn't go down without a fight—a fight that would not be worth it. He'd see to that.

He gave them a wide berth, wary of any of their associates who might lurk nearby. The men let him pass without harassment, but Aaron's unease did not abate. Instead, it grew stronger with every yard he traveled. Lacy would have to pass those same men. She had said she didn't need him to walk her home, but…

He stopped and looked back. His gut churned with a warning of something sinister at play, and he couldn't ignore it. The least he could do was make sure Lacy made it past the men unmolested. She couldn't deny him that.

He strode back toward the tavern, picking up speed as he neared the corner where he had seen the men. They were gone when he arrived, but a muffled cry echoed from an alley down the side street. Aaron's mouth went dry, and he sprinted toward the sound. He skidded to a halt in the alley. His thrashing heart exploded in fury as his vision narrowed in on two men who had Lacy pressed up against a wall, taunting and jeering as she struggled against them.

Adrenaline spiking, Aaron reached out and grabbed the nearest man by the back of his coat. He yanked him away from Lacy and slammed him against the opposite building. The second man turned. Aaron ducked under a widely thrown punch. He landed his own blow right to the man's gut and sent him sprawling. The first man jumped to his partner's aid and caught Aaron with a glancing blow to the chin. Their wild and badly aimed swings marked them as average street thugs and not experienced fighters.

It took only a brief couple of minutes for Aaron to have them both crawling away on their hands and knees. He reached down for the nearest one's collar and forced the man to look up at him.

"If either of you ever cross paths with her again, you won't even be able to crawl, do you understand?"

The man didn't answer, but his cowed posture was enough. Aaron let him go.

"Now get out of here."

The men hobbled to their feet and slunk away, holding handfuls of snow to their bruised faces. Satisfied they wouldn't try anything foolish, Aaron spun around.

Lacy huddled next to the wall, staring at him with huge eyes. Aaron knelt in front of her. All his anger melted into concern.

"Are you all right?"

She was breathing hard and didn't seem to have a voice, but she nodded. After another moment, she said breathlessly, "Yes, I'm all right."

Aaron gripped her arms gently and helped her to her feet. Her cloak was all twisted around her shoulders, and he helped her straighten it. She looked up at him, her eyes still rounded and a little too wet. Aaron fought the burning desire to go after the men again. He could only pray they would heed his warning. Heaven help them if they didn't.

"Why don't I walk you the rest of the way home?"

This time, she nodded. He put his hand to her back and guided her out of the alley. She gripped her cloak close to her throat and didn't speak for over a block and a half. Aaron couldn't blame her. Those men probably would have had their way and then killed her. That's the way things were now in Valcré. People turned up dead all the time in the name of the queen's false gods.

At last, Lacy's voice broke free. "Thank you."

He looked down into her timid gaze. "I'm just glad I came back." Thank Elôm he hadn't dismissed the internal warning as paranoia.

"You came back?"

Aaron nodded. "I passed the men when I left the tavern. I knew you would too. The farther I went, the more I felt I should come back to make sure you were all right."

Lacy released a trembling breath. "I'm usually more aware of potential danger, but I didn't notice them until it was too late. I think they were waiting there for me."

Aaron frowned. They had targeted her specifically? "Why?"

"When they dragged me into the alley, they said Victor charges too much for my…" she hesitated and cleared her throat, "services. They didn't want to pay."

She ducked her head and hunched her shoulders. He studied her guilt-ridden profile. It was probably the attack, but she seemed more pale than usual. Every fiber and bone in his body ached to protect her. If only the circumstances were different.

"Well, I don't think they'll be hanging around again," Aaron tried to comfort her and prayed Elôm would place a shield of protection around her. Now, more than ever, he couldn't stand the thought of her traveling alone. But he couldn't be with her every time. It just wasn't possible, and even if she allowed it, it wasn't his place. He would do all he could for her, but she wasn't his to protect.

They walked the rest of the way in silence. When they

reached a house similar to yet smaller than the one Aaron shared with the others, Lacy stopped.

"This is it."

Aaron eyed the candlelit windows. At least Lacy had a warm and inviting home to return to after work.

The curtains on one of the windows near the door parted. A female face peeked out at them. About in her late-teens, she looked like a young version of Lacy. For the first time since they'd left the tavern, a smile reached Lacy's lips.

"That's my youngest sister, Gwen. I'm sure she'll want to know all about this." She turned her smile to him, though it lost a little of its vibrancy. "Thank you again. I can't tell you how grateful I am."

"I'm just thankful Elôm brought me back there." He studied her expression. She didn't display any hostility toward his faith, but she didn't openly embrace it either. "If you ever want to come to one of the meetings, just let me know. I'll be around."

"I will."

She then turned and walked up the short path to the house. He waited until she stepped inside and gave him one more brief smile before closing the door.

Stuffing his hands in his pockets, he set off in the direction of the warehouse meeting hall. While he should be getting mentally prepared for Timothy's message, his thoughts lingered on Lacy. He wouldn't sleep well tonight knowing she would head to work alone in the morning.

His mood matched the deepening shadows when he arrived at the warehouse. Candles and lanterns lit up the open interior. Only a couple of people had arrived so far, including Ben. A month ago, they'd filled the warehouse with those sick from Miner's Fever. Thankfully, all had recovered once they'd received the remedy.

Trading a greeting with Ben and the others, Aaron walked over to Timothy. His younger brother sat at a table at the far end of the building in front of a grouping of benches and chairs. Timothy looked up with a smile, but it slowly faded.

"She's not coming?"

Aaron shook his head. "No, she wants to be with her mother and sisters. I can't blame her, but that's not the problem." He sank into a chair next to Timothy and recounted the attack in the alley.

"I wish I could do something." Aaron sighed when he finished. Timothy might be a full twelve years younger than him, but, at times like this, his little brother seemed significantly wiser. Aaron could use any bit of wisdom right now.

Timothy didn't respond immediately. He just watched Aaron for a moment before finally speaking. "You've fallen for her, haven't you?"

Aaron slumped in his chair. He had shrugged off his interest in Lacy with Jace and Holden, but his brother deserved the truth. It wasn't as if he didn't see it already anyway.

"Hard."

He had never anticipated what visiting the tavern for information would lead to. She had caught his eye right away, not with typical attraction, but with her smile that, for some reason, turned so sweet and genuine when she saw him. It was as if she had sensed in that first encounter that he was not like the other men who frequented the tavern.

Ever since then, he'd wanted nothing more than to see her happy and smiling all the time, and not those fake, paid-for smiles she gave while working. He'd never believed himself to be the type of man to fall so hard for someone—he'd always thought himself far more practical and sensible than that—but he couldn't get Lacy out of his head, and didn't particularly want to.

That's where the danger lay. The desire to protect her was one thing, but to pursue her romantically when she did not follow Elôm, and perhaps never would, was folly. He couldn't compromise his faith no matter how strong his feelings might be or how painful it was not to act on them.

Timothy offered him a sympathetic smile. After all, he had dealt with his own complicated relationship. "I'll pray for her safety. And keep praying she and her family will come to our meetings or at least be open to hearing about Elôm if you have the opportunity to speak to them."

He paused, and his smile changed to a look of brotherly concern. "I'll pray for you too."

Aaron understood everything behind those quiet words. He had dedicated his life to following Elôm, but he wasn't so arrogant as to think he was infallible. He knew the pitfalls and snares he would have to navigate in this situation. Timothy would help keep him accountable.

"Thanks."

A smile returned to Timothy's face. "Maybe I can visit Lacy's family. If they come to know Elôm, she would have a lot more exposure to Him, even without coming to the meetings."

Hope grew in Aaron's heart stronger than he had felt in a while. If anyone could lead Lacy's family to faith in Elôm, it was his brother. Timothy had a way with words that Aaron did not.

Timothy dipped his quill into the inkpot on his desk and finished the final paragraph of his letter for those back in Landale. He would send it with the next messenger who visited Valcré. Of course, he hoped the messenger would be Leetra. It had been difficult to say goodbye after Kyrin and Jace's wedding. Elôm willing, and if she accepted, perhaps she would come to Valcré, not as a messenger, but to stay. Whatever the future held, he had a personal letter ready for her just in case she wasn't Trask's next messenger.

Setting the camp letter aside to dry, he leaned back in his chair and looked out the window. Sunlight filtered through the frosted panes. Glorious sunlight. When the sun shone, the bleakness and evil in the city didn't seem quite so heavy. It was the perfect opportunity to get out and see to things. He sat for a moment of prayer for guidance and then pushed to his feet.

In the entryway, he pulled on his boots and buckled on a sword before slipping into his coat. Aaron wouldn't be keen on him heading out alone, but Timothy wasn't without skill when it came to a blade.

He stepped into their small kitchen and left a quick note for Aaron to let him know where he'd gone in case he returned before Timothy did. After that, he braved the cold, pleasantly surprised to find it didn't have the bitter bite it usually did. If nothing else, he was glad for Aaron's sake. Most days he spent working outside at the docks. Though there wasn't as much work as when the ships weren't ice-locked, there were always odd jobs for men willing to do hard work. And hard meant exhausting. There were some evenings Aaron returned home so worn out it reminded Timothy of their days in Dunlow. He prayed springtime would bring less grueling opportunities.

Turning his thoughts toward his mission, Timothy set off down the street. He had spent a lot of time contemplating his conversation with Aaron at the warehouse two nights ago. He'd known even before they talked that Aaron had developed feelings for Lacy. It was difficult for Timothy to balance his joy that his brother may have found love with his concern over the situation in which he'd found it. Aaron was smart and one of the most loyal and responsible men Timothy knew. He didn't believe his brother would make a wrong or unwise choice, but he was afraid to see his brother's heart broken.

Aaron had dedicated his life to looking out for Timothy. It was time he had someone to love and share his life with who wasn't his brother. He deserved to have a woman at his side. Especially if things continued to progress between Timothy and Leetra. Aaron wouldn't know what to do with himself after all this time if Timothy got married. He breathed out a chuckle. It was definitely time they both moved on from their bachelor lives and had their own families to care for.

Lord, please work in Aaron's life. Above all, give him wisdom and the strength to honor You, even if it means a broken heart. But, if it is Your will, work things out between him and Lacy. Draw her to Your truth and soften her heart to accept it. Bring her out of the life she is in now and let her see Your forgiveness. I know that is what Aaron wants above anything else.

Timothy prayed for his brother and Lacy all the way until he reached the address Aaron had given him. He paused at the walkway of the house and whispered a prayer for wisdom and guidance for himself. This could play a large part in Aaron's future with Lacy, depending on how this visit went.

Knowing Elôm was at his side and that every soul was precious, he followed the path to the door and knocked. He peered over his shoulder for any hint of trouble, but he swung his gaze back around when the door opened. A woman stood on the other side. Gray streaked her dark hair, though her face was still relatively free of wrinkles. Timothy met her eyes and read fear in them, though she masked it well.

"Can I help you?"

"Mrs. Evern?" Timothy inquired gently. He kept his hand clear of his sword. Any woman living without protection in this city had a right to be wary of strangers at their door.

"Yes?" Her tone was more guarded now, her mask slipping just a bit.

"I am Timothy Silvar. My brother, Aaron, is friends with Lacy."

The woman's face relaxed, the release of tension smoothing it once again. "Is everything all right with Aaron? We have not met him, but Lacy has told us much about him."

Timothy smiled to assure her. "Aaron is fine. I know how difficult times are for so many in in the city, and I thought I would drop by to see how your family is doing."

A soft smile grew on Mrs. Evern's face. Aaron had mentioned Lacy's genuine smile. It must be something she had inherited from her mother.

"That is very kind of you." She moved back a half a step. "Would you like to come in, out of the cold?"

"If it's no inconvenience to you. I don't wish to impose."

She shook her head. "It's no imposition. We rarely have company, so a guest would be a welcome change."

Timothy slipped into the small entry, taking in the sparse furnishings. Mrs. Evern then offered to take his coat, and he shrugged it off. He also unbuckled his sword and rested it against the wall. No need to give a threatening appearance here.

"Why don't you come into the kitchen? It's much warmer there."

Timothy followed her through a door just to the left. When they entered the room, he saw two young women. The older of the two, who appeared to be around his age, sat at the table with a book, while the younger one sat near the fireplace.

"These are two of my daughters—Hannah and Gwen." Mrs. Evern introduced him to the pair, and he greeted them kindly. "Lacy went out to get a few things for supper." She then motioned to the table. "Please, sit."

Timothy accepted the invitation and pulled out the chair opposite Hannah. He took stock of the kitchen as he sat down. It was as sparse as the entry, and the cupboards were noticeably bare. Thanks to experience, he could spot a struggling family when he saw one.

"Would you like some tea?" Mrs. Evern asked.

Timothy looked to her inquiring face. To offer him anything would surely deplete what little they had. He held up his hand. "Please, I don't wish to be a burden. I know how hard this winter has been for everyone."

Mrs. Evern gave him a gently insistent look. "We won't starve over one cup of tea."

Timothy smiled and nodded. "Then I would love some."

The woman lifted a kettle from where it hung near the fireplace and poured it into a mug of tea leaves. A strong but pleasant aroma filled the kitchen. Peppermint. That had been Josan's favorite. He used to—

Mrs. Evern reached out to grip the table and pressed her other hand to her chest. She pulled in a breath, but it wheezed into her lungs. Timothy started to rise, but Gwen jumped up from her seat and grabbed a small vial from a shelf. She placed it in her mother's waiting hand, and Mrs. Evern breathed in whatever herbs or medicinal concoction it contained. After a couple more wheezing breaths, the malady that had taken hold subsided.

She gave Gwen a weak smile. "Thank you."

Timothy looked between them and then focused on Mrs. Evern. "Are you all right?"

She fluttered her hand in dismissal. "I'm fine. It's a lung condition I've had since I was a child. Cold weather makes it worse."

Timothy settled back down in his chair. This family had even more hardships to endure than was first apparent. Did Aaron know of Mrs. Evern's condition?

She set his tea before him, along with a small bowl of sugar. Timothy thanked her and spooned just a little of the sugar into his cup.

Mrs. Evern sat down next to Hannah, curiosity lighting her eyes. "Have you and Aaron always lived in Valcré?"

Timothy shook his head and told them about growing up in the Graylin Valley. The moment he mentioned their crete heritage, Gwen joined them at the table. She had many questions, especially when she learned that he had visited Arvael. Her bubbly personality and inquisitive nature reminded him of Talas's sister, Trenna. Though much quieter than her sister, Hannah was just as intrigued, judging by her riveted expression. She was definitely the bookworm of the family. Though Timothy couldn't see exactly what she was reading, it looked like an adventure novel. He had read a few of those growing up when he wasn't reading the Scrolls. It was a way to learn about the world outside of the Graylin Valley.

This easy conversation helped him get to know the Evern women and for them to trust and feel comfortable with him. By the time he finished his tea, he felt a tugging to broach more serious topics. He prayed internally for the right words and that their hearts would be open to receiving them. Lacy knew that Aaron was a follower of Elôm, but did her family? Even if they were not opposed, the price on his head as a member of the Resistance would be tempting to anyone in their situation. But he let those concerns rest in Elôm's hands. Elôm had given him a voice to reach people. To keep silent in the face of danger would not only be wasting a precious gift, but turning his back on souls in dire need of Elôm's love.

"I don't know if she has ever mentioned it, but Aaron has invited Lacy to the gatherings we have with some others from around the city." He watched Mrs. Evern's face intently for a reaction. It was easy to spot those who were opposed or frightened of faith in Elôm.

However, the woman just nodded in interest rather than opposition or fear. "You are Elôm followers."

Timothy answered without hesitation. "Yes."

She nodded slowly, as if mulling it over. "We were never ones to follow Aertus and Vilai. Before he died, my husband Isaac was intrigued by what he heard of Elôm, but we never really looked into it because of the danger."

"It is dangerous," Timothy said honestly. "My uncle was murdered because of his faith and the father of one of my close friends was executed right here in Valcré. But I can tell you with certainty that neither one of them would have chosen to believe differently if they were given a second chance. Our faith is not simply an acknowledgement of a higher power or a struggle to appease and gain favor through sacrifices. It's a relationship full of love as with a child and their father."

He had their interest now. A longing shone in their eyes,

especially in Gwen and Hannah's, perhaps since they'd been without a father for the last couple of years.

With another prayer for wisdom, Timothy shared Elôm's love and the sacrifice Elon had made. He told stories of how his father had taught him and his experiences in living out his faith. Mrs. Evern and her daughters listened much more openly than many people Timothy had witnessed to. He wasn't sure if they listened with genuine interest or simply politeness, but at least the door was open.

He took care not to talk too much or overlong, leaving them with the essentials of faith and salvation without overwhelming them. When he finished, he said, "You are all welcome to join our meetings. Everyone is welcoming and quick to help one another. I know it's dangerous, but once you get to know Elôm and how much He loves us, it's a risk we're willing to take. And willing to risk sharing with others as well."

"I have encouraged Lacy to go if she wants," Mrs. Evern said.

This was a good sign. She wouldn't have encouraged her daughter if she were opposed to it.

"Hannah and Gwen are free to attend if they wish," she continued, "but I'm afraid I wouldn't be able to go out until the weather is warmer."

Timothy nodded in full understanding. "If you'd like, I could stop by once in a while and share some of the teaching from our meetings. I don't wish to intrude, so it's entirely your choice."

Mrs. Evern smiled kindly. "I think I'd like that if it's no inconvenience or added danger to you. I can see why my husband was interested in Elôm." She drew a breath, sorrow ghosting across her face. "There's not much to offer hope these days."

Timothy understood the sentiment. After his father had died and Aaron had spent almost every waking hour working to provide for them, he'd felt the same way at times.

"I know how that feels. I also know from experience that Elôm is always near to offer hope and peace."

A thirst for such peace welled in the woman's eyes, and Timothy's heart rejoiced with the certainty that Elôm was at work here.

"Next time I visit," he said, "I'll bring you copies of some of the verses from the King's Scrolls. One of the best ways to get to know Elôm is by reading His Word."

Hannah perked up at this. Already Timothy determined to spend his evening gathering and copying verses that would be of particular benefit to this family. He had a few letters written that would also be good for them.

The front door opened, interrupting the conversation. Timothy looked over his shoulder. Another woman in her mid to late twenties stepped into the kitchen, a basket clutched in front of her. Though Timothy had never seen her before, he knew at once it was Lacy. She looked a lot like her mother and sisters, especially Gwen.

Her gaze connected with his, her weary expression going taut. Fear flashed in her eyes, not quite concealed by the hard and determined mask she slipped into place. She appeared ready to do battle while at the same time expecting to lose.

"This is Aaron's brother, Timothy," her mother said.

Lacy's mask fell away as relief poured in. She repeated his name.

He rose from his chair and faced her with a smile. Even standing a little less than average in height, he still found her a couple of inches shorter than he was. The perfect height for Aaron. He brushed the thought away. A lot would have to change before that would be acceptable.

"I'm pleased to meet you," he told her. "Aaron speaks of you fondly."

Lacy glanced down at the floor, her cheeks tinged pink. She smiled as she looked up at him again, though it was strained with weariness.

"Aaron has spoken very fondly of you as well."

Timothy's smile grew. He could see why Aaron was smitten, but it was more than her pretty face. Everything about her begged to be cared for and protected despite how she fought to hide her vulnerability. He didn't have to be Kyrin Altair to see how the choices she'd had to make weighed on her.

Though he would have liked to speak with her more, he felt it was time to leave. He didn't want to wear out his welcome, and Lacy looked like she needed rest. Stepping back so that she could set the basket on the table, he turned to her mother.

"It's getting late. I had better go. Aaron will be home soon, and he'll no doubt worry if I'm gone."

Mrs. Evern gave a nod. "I'll get your coat."

After saying goodbye to her and her daughters, Timothy left the house and walked briskly back to his own. The visit had gone even better than he'd hoped. Aaron would be pleased. Hopefully Mrs. Evern and the other girls would talk to Lacy about their conversations. He could see her having a harder time accepting it. She was clearly the provider of the family now, just as Aaron had always been after the mining accident. If she was anything like his brother, she would be wary of something that could bring such danger to her family. Obviously, she was willing to go to great lengths to protect and provide for them.

When he reached home, he opened the door and found Aaron waiting in the entry. No doubt he had checked out the window every five minutes to look for Timothy and debated whether or not to come after him. A smile tugged at Timothy's lips. He didn't dismiss the danger in the city, but his brother was overly protective at times.

Timothy slipped off his coat and turned to hang it on a peg next to his brother's.

"Well?"

Perhaps his brother wasn't so much worried but chomping at the bit to find out about his visit. Timothy turned to face him as he unbuckled his sword. He wouldn't torture his brother by drawing this out.

"It was a very good visit. Lacy's mother and sisters were very open to learning about Elôm. I'm going to take them some of the Scrolls, probably tomorrow." Timothy pried off his boots and slid them up against the wall. "I enjoyed getting to know them. They're very kind."

Aaron smiled, but then his expression turned questioning. "Was Lacy there?"

"Not until just before I left. She was out shopping, so I didn't get a chance to talk to her."

Aaron nodded as he took this in. He looked caught between being pleased at how things had gone with Lacy's family and disappointed that Timothy hadn't spoken to her.

"Once they have the Scrolls, she'll be able to read them if she wants. Her mother has also encouraged her to attend the meetings."

This lifted Aaron's expression. "So, how was she?"

"Well, I can see why you like her." Timothy gave his brother a knowing smile and clapped him on the shoulder as he made his way into the kitchen. "She's pretty."

He opened one of the cupboards and pulled out ingredients for supper. It was their turn to prepare it, although Aaron was a terrible cook, so most of it would be up to Timothy. He glanced over his shoulder. Aaron had a not-very-well concealed smile on his face.

"Did she seem well?" he amended his question.

Timothy grew more serious. "It's the first time I've seen her, but she seemed pale."

Any lingering trace of Aaron's smile disappeared.

"It may have been fear," Timothy said. "She was definitely afraid until her mother introduced me. I think she thought I was someone else. Her mother had the same reaction when she answered the door."

Aaron remained silent for a long moment, lost in whatever thoughts occupied his mind. Finally, he snapped out of it. "Do you think they'll maintain their interest in Elôm?"

Timothy filled a pot with water to boil rice. "Unless something scares them off, I would think so. Especially once I give them the Scrolls. Lacy's middle sister, Hannah, loves to read."

It certainly was good news for Aaron. Better than either of them had expected, but Timothy's thoughts turned to a specific moment in his discussion with Mrs. Evern.

"How did Mr. Evern die?"

"The physician said his heart gave out."

Timothy drew his brows together. "Was anyone with him when he died?"

Aaron matched his frown. "I don't think so. I think they found him dead in one of his shops. Why?"

Timothy shook his head. "It probably has nothing to do with it, but Mrs. Evern said he had an interest in Elôm."

"You think he might have been killed because of it?"

"I have no idea. It was just a thought I had."

He dumped the rice into the pot and hung it over the fireplace. Aaron was silent behind him as he laid a couple of chunks of wood on the coals. He brushed his hands on his pants and turned back to his brother. Aaron had a thoughtful look in his eyes.

"Do you think he could have believed in Elôm before he died?"

Timothy shrugged. "It depends on how great his interest was and how much he learned. Who knows what he was thinking or what decisions he made in his final moments. He could have placed his faith in Elôm."

WITH WORKING LATE at the docks, Aaron hadn't had a chance to see Lacy since he'd walked her home the other night. He was incredibly grateful to Timothy for visiting her family yesterday, but one thing just wouldn't leave his mind—Timothy's observation of how pale Lacy had been. Hadn't Aaron thought the same thing last time he saw her? Of course, it could just be fear, but something in his gut didn't accept that answer. And why did Lacy and her mother have such a fearful reaction to Timothy? Who had they feared he was?

Whether he would gain any answers to these questions or not, Aaron determined to check on her today. He finished his work early and didn't wait around to see if there was extra to be done like he normally did. He could do that tomorrow. Having built up a reputation as a hard laborer, he didn't usually have trouble finding work when he needed it.

It was a long walk from the docks to the tavern, but the weariness of the trip and long day of work eased when he arrived. He shouldn't be so eager, but his emotions weren't as quick to comply with his common sense. With a prayer, he pushed open the door and stepped in. The buzz of voices was especially loud today. A couple of large groups occupied the tables scattered around the common room, and the rest were taken up by two or three men each. He spotted only one table not in use. Then he caught sight of Lacy serving a group at the back. When she turned and spotted him, her face lifted a little but didn't reach a smile. Her expression was too frazzled for that.

As the other barmaids bustled about, Aaron made his way up to the bar where Victor busily filled mugs. Aaron drew a coin from his pocket and set it on the counter. Victor handed off a tray to one of the girls and then turned to Aaron. He didn't look particularly pleased to see him, but asked, "The usual?"

Aaron nodded, and Victor filled him a mug of ale that Aaron carried to the empty table. He sipped absently as he watched Lacy tend one table after another. It took almost a half an hour before she finally gained a chance to make her way over to him. He smiled at her, but the one she offered in exchange did not light up her face as it normally did. Aaron's slowly died, and he observed her strained expression and tired eyes. Had she been crying?

He set his mug aside and leaned forward. "Are you all right?"

She dropped her gaze. "I'm fine."

Aaron didn't believe that for a moment.

Lacy lifted her face again, a mask in place. "My mother and sisters enjoyed your brother's visit."

Aaron peered up at her, not giving much thought to her comment. It was an obvious attempt to divert attention away from herself. "He enjoyed it too."

He searched her eyes for answers. This time, she didn't look away. The mask started to slip.

"Hey, Silvar."

Aaron jerked at Victor's gruff voice carrying from the bar.

"If you're going to keep taking up her time, you can pay for it."

Aaron shot him a glare. By the time he looked back at Lacy, the mask was intact again.

"I should get back to work." She turned and hurried to the bar before he had a chance to breathe another word.

Aaron forced out a hard sigh and sent another dour look Victor's way. If he was going to find out anything from Lacy, it wouldn't be with her employer around. He reached for his mug and gulped down the last swallow of ale. Lacy didn't get off early tonight, so he wouldn't have the opportunity to talk to her after work. Something was wrong, and the idea of just leaving churned like spoiled meat in his stomach.

Pewter and glass crashed to the floor. Aaron stiffened, his gaze darting to Lacy. A crestfallen look crossed her face just before she knelt next to the tray that must have slipped from her hands. Foaming ale ran along the floorboards from the overturned mugs, and shards of a ceramic bowl stuck out of an oozing puddle of stew.

Aaron shoved to his feet and rushed to her side. "Let me help you."

He reached for a piece of the bowl and set it on the tray. She said nothing, but when he looked up and met her eyes, they nearly overflowed with tears. He'd never seen her cry before, or her eyes so tormented. This had nothing to do with a dropped tray. Aaron's protectiveness burst to life like a blast of dragon fire. He didn't care who he had to face, he would fix whatever was wrong. He opened his mouth to speak, but Victor cut him off.

"Silvar!"

Aaron held Lacy's gaze a moment longer and then straightened. He strode toward the bar. Reaching into his pocket, he pulled out the handful of coins he'd earned today and slapped them down on the counter with a cold look at Victor. The coins would more than cover what Aaron had heard the man charged for Lacy's company.

Without a word, he returned to her side and touched her arm. Damp streaks glistened on her cheeks.

"Let's go talk," he told her gently.

He helped her to her feet, and she glanced around as if unsure or hesitant. Biting her lip, she turned, and Aaron followed her upstairs. He knew how condemning this looked, but right now, his concern was for Lacy.

Six closed doors lined the dim hall at the top of the stairs. Lacy opened the first one, and they stepped into an equally dim room. Twilight leaked around a dark curtain hanging in front of one window. Aaron glanced around. The room was small—just large enough for a washstand, a chair, and a bed.

Lacy closed the door and lit a candle. As the small, wavering flame lit the room, she turned to face him but wouldn't meet his eyes. She shifted and rubbed her arms.

"I just want to talk," Aaron assured her.

He motioned to the chair, and she sat down, smoothing her skirt over her knees. Aaron remained standing at the foot of the bed, but her gaze darted around as if she were trapped and seeking an escape. Or maybe it was this room and what it meant to her.

"What's wrong, Lacy?"

She finally looked up at him, and their eyes locked. Fear and despair flashed through hers. Then her whole body sagged as if the strength holding her together vanished. Her eyes filled with tears again. Aaron barely caught the words that murmured past her lips.

"I'm pregnant."

Aaron's jaw fell open, and he stared at where her hand rested over her stomach. She was going to have a baby? Though he hadn't noticed before, now that he was looking for it, he did see how she filled out the middle of her dress. Of all the scenarios he'd imagined and prepared for, this was not one of them. He had no plan for this.

"When Victor finds out, he'll make me get rid of it."

Her words simultaneously snapped him from distress over how to help her to recoiling over the shock of what she implied. He looked her in the eyes again. Teardrops quivered on her lashes now. She swiped at them.

"I should've taken care of it when I first found out. I know I should have, but—"

Her words ripped at Aaron's heart, propelling him forward. He knelt in front of her chair.

"No, no. You were right not to."

Lacy shook her head, the tears finally trailing down her cheeks. "But I can't keep working if I don't. Victor won't allow it."

Aaron ground his teeth. No one would make Lacy give up her baby. Not if he had anything to say about it.

"How far along are you?"

Lacy sniffed. "About six and a half months."

Aaron raised his brows. He didn't know much about pregnancy, but shouldn't she be bigger by now?

"I started showing late," Lacy said. "I just started filling out recently. I've hidden it, but I don't think I can for much longer. Victor will notice."

Aaron breathed out slowly. He didn't have a plan for this, but he would make one. "Does your mother know?"

Lacy nodded, a sob breaking free. "She doesn't want to lose the baby, but I have no choice."

"Yes, you do."

Lacy shook her head. "No, I don't."

"You can quit."

Her face scrunched up like she was in great pain, and her shoulders shook. "I can't," she cried.

She drooped forward again, burying her face in her hands as she sobbed. Aaron watched, fighting every screaming impulse to pull her close and hold her and tell her he would take care of everything.

He cleared his throat. "Lacy."

She didn't seem to hear him. He tried again, but when she still wouldn't respond, he reached out and touched her hands. Finally, she looked up, her lips trembling. Aaron gently brushed away the hair clinging to her wet cheeks.

"Listen to me." He rested his hand against the side of her head. "You can quit. I will take care of you and your family until we figure things out. You don't have to stay here."

He'd wanted to offer this a long time ago. He hadn't been sure he should then, but he had to now.

Still, Lacy's tears fell heavily. "No." She choked back a sob. "It won't work."

"Why not?"

"It won't be enough."

She shook her head again, and Aaron waited as she seemed to get a hold of herself. She breathed in hard, and the tears slowed as she stared at him.

"It's not just food and necessities we need. It's my father's debt. If I don't keep paying it off, my mother will end up in the workhouse." Her voice broke. "She would never survive."

No wonder Lacy had taken this job. Timothy had told him about Mrs. Evern's lung condition. Some healthy men didn't even survive the workhouses.

"How much do you owe?"

Lacy bowed her head, her expression strained. She didn't speak for a long moment, and heaviness built in Aaron's stomach.

At last, she whispered, "Almost three hundred pounds."

Aaron couldn't stop a wince. Three hundred pounds? He had been lucky to make twenty a year working six days a week in the mines.

Lacy's voice trembled as she continued, "My father borrowed money to expand his business. I tried to keep it running, but it all fell apart. By the time I sold everything and paid everyone who had invested, there wasn't enough to cover the debt."

Aaron ground his teeth together. Hadn't she had anyone to help her? "Who do you owe the money to?"

"A man named Mr. Darwin."

Aaron nodded slowly. He'd heard the name before.

Apparently, he was one of the wealthiest businessmen in the city, and not someone who would overlook such a debt.

"I've never met him," Lacy went on. "He has a debt collector, Banson, working for him. He or one of his men always comes to collect the money."

Debt collectors. Things clicked into place. That's why Lacy and her family reacted in fear toward Timothy.

"Have they threatened you?"

Lacy's lips pinched, and she nodded. "Sometimes, when we are a little short on our payments, Banson threatens to take my mother if I don't have more next time."

Ire prickled inside Aaron, and he itched to get his hands on this Banson. He'd known similar men back in Dunlow. They had no pity when it came to collecting money.

Lacy sniffed again, and her voice held resignation. "Now you see. I can't keep this baby because I can't quit."

Her eyes were so tortured that Aaron couldn't help himself. He reached out and took her hand. She didn't pull away.

"No," he said, looking her in the eyes. "This doesn't change anything. I'll take on the debt." It was a heavy burden to accept, but he would do it willingly.

Lacy shook her head. "It's too much. I can't make you do that."

He squeezed her hand. "You're not. I'm making the decision. The most important thing to me right now is protecting the baby."

Lacy wavered, indecision warring in her eyes.

Aaron took her hand in both of his now. "Lacy, you don't have to do this anymore. You can walk away from this place and never come back. All you have to do is let me help you."

A little sob escaped as longing engulfed her whole face. "I want to, but I can't just go. Victor won't let me. I've had to borrow money from him for some payments. I can't go until I pay it off."

"How much?"

"Two pounds."

Aaron couldn't help a little smile. Next to her father's debt, what she owed Victor was the least of their problems.

"I'll go get the money right now. You can walk out of here today and put it behind you for good." He paused, searching her eyes. "If that is what you want."

He held his breath.

After only a moment, she nodded, fresh tears cascading down her cheeks. "Yes." She slipped her hand out of his and covered her face, crying softly as if a huge burden were falling away. Through her fingers, she murmured, "Thank you!"

Aaron put his hand on her shoulder and rubbed it gently. She let her hands fall from her face and then leaned forward, wrapping her arms around Aaron's neck. Aaron closed his arms around her, holding her as she cried. His heart walloped his chest. If he wasn't careful, she would unknowingly steal it completely.

With an adorable hiccup, she pulled back a few moments later and wiped her face. The heavy cosmetics she wore smeared around her eyes and smudged her cheeks. She was a mess, but it only tugged at Aaron's heart all the more. She drew a couple of deep breaths and composed herself. Once the tears had stopped, she said a bit hoarsely, "Thank you."

Aaron smiled at her. He had wanted to do this for so long. "Happy to help."

He stood up and helped Lacy to her feet. She started wiping her face again, the cosmetics staining her fingers.

"I'm sorry. I must look terrible."

Aaron shook his head. "No." He couldn't tell her how he thought the exact opposite. He cleared his throat and focused on the matter at hand. He'd been in here long enough.

"I'll go get the money and come right back to take you home."

Lacy nodded, and Aaron turned. At the door, he paused and glanced back.

"Lacy, as of right now, you don't have to do any of this ever again."

AARON WASTED NO time in retrieving the money he had been saving since starting to work in Valcré. He hadn't even told Timothy what he was doing, only promising to explain later as he'd rushed from the house. He didn't know why the matter felt so urgent, but he didn't want Lacy to spend one more minute in that tavern. And the baby. Heavens, how had she kept that a secret for so long? Thank Elôm that she had allowed Aaron to help her. Whatever he had to do, he would see that little one born safe and sound.

When he arrived back at the tavern, he spotted Lacy near the bar. Her tense expression put Aaron on alert. The moment she noticed him, relief washed over her face. That's when Aaron noticed an impatient-looking brute hovering nearby and Victor standing in front of Lacy with a scowl. Ire burned through Aaron, and he strode across the room.

"As long as you work for me, you'll do as you're told," Victor told Lacy with a growl. When he realized that she wasn't paying attention to him, he turned and found Aaron. His scowl deepened. "What are you doing back here?"

Aaron brushed past the lout eycing Lacy and faced down Victor. "She doesn't have to take orders from you anymore." He reached into his coat and withdrew a heavy bag of coins. "This is what she owes you. She's done working here."

Victor gaped at him. "You can't just come in here and do this. Is this even what she wants?"

He fixed a demanding gaze on Lacy. She glanced between the two of them. Fear stabbed Aaron at the uncertainty that flashed in her eyes, but then she drew herself up and spoke softly.

"Yes, Victor, it is."

He just stared at her for a moment, and then shook his head with a grumble. Aaron stepped closer to Lacy.

"Do you need to get anything?"

"My coat," she murmured. "I'll get it."

She turned and disappeared up the stairs.

"But I already paid for an hour with her," the man behind Aaron complained.

Aaron spun around and speared him with a searing look. As if Lacy were nothing more than an object at the beck and call of any man's whim. Though half a foot taller than Aaron, the man shrank a little. Good thing too. Aaron was about ready to punch him in the nose if he'd persisted.

Mumbling darkly under his breath, Victor went to the bar and returned the man's money. As the patron shambled away, Victor turned on Aaron with a look that suggested he wished he had a weapon in hand.

Aaron would gladly have gone toe-to-toe with him, but he kept his ire in check. "Lacy is not a commodity."

Still fuming, Victor turned away and stalked behind the bar. A moment later, Tess slipped over to Aaron. She lowered her voice, though there was nothing seductive about it this time.

"You take care of our girl, you hear? You're doing real good by her, but make sure you don't end up just leaving her to fend for herself." Surprisingly, she had the protective look of a mother bear.

Aaron nodded. "I won't, I promise."

The protective look turned to satisfaction. "Good. She deserves better than this."

Tess had always seemed to have a soft spot toward Lacy. Aaron had to wonder how she had ended up in this life. Had she found herself in dire straits as a young woman just as Lacy had? Clearly no one had come along to help her out of it.

Footsteps tapped the stairs lightly, and he turned as Lacy joined them again, this time wearing her coat. She gave Victor a hesitant look. "I'm sorry you didn't have more warning."

Victor just glowered at her.

Aaron slipped his arm around her and guided her toward the door. They hadn't gone far when Victor called after them.

"Once you pass that door, you're on your own. There's only one job women can get in this city, and you won't find anywhere that treats you as well as you had it here. You'd better think hard about how you're going to support your mother and sisters."

Lacy slowed, and Aaron murmured, "Don't listen to him."

She kept going, but her body felt rigid. When they stepped outside, a shiver passed through her, though Aaron didn't know if it was the cold or Victor's words. They walked in silence for a couple of blocks until Lacy stopped suddenly. Aaron halted and looked down at her. She stared straight ahead, her eyes wide, but not focused on anything tangible. A tremor passed through her again.

"I can't do this," she gasped. She turned, her wide, panicked eyes on him now, and shook her head. "I have to go back. Victor is right. How can I take care of them? I don't have anywhere else to go."

Aaron gripped her arms firmly but gently, willing her to calm down. "Lacy, I already told you, I will take care of things until we figure this out."

"But Mr. Darwin. His debt collector will come by any day now. I have almost nothing to give him. If he finds out I quit, he'll—"

"Lacy."

She stopped and stared up at him, the fear racing through her eyes barely slowing down.

"I have enough for you to give him." Aaron touched his coat where he had another pouch of coins. He looked deeply in her eyes. "Everything will be all right."

She didn't even blink for a moment, but then she let out a breath that seemed to deflate the panic. Her eyes still held fear, though trust joined it. Slowly, she nodded, entrusting her life and her family to him. It was a weighty burden, yet he was more than happy to take it from her.

Aaron motioned down the street, and they started

walking again. When she seemed to breathe more evenly, he asked, "Is there anything you need for the baby?"

She was silent for a long moment. "Clothes." She shrugged. "I haven't given it much thought. I didn't think I would ever be able to keep it."

She put her hand to her stomach as if just now realizing she was a mother. That surely brought a fresh slew of uncertainties and fear. Aaron kept his voice light to encourage her.

"That will be easily fixed. We have a large group of women in our congregation who would be happy to provide clothing and supplies for you."

She glanced up at him. "Are you sure of that once they know where the baby came from?"

"A baby is a baby. That's all that matters." Sure, some might judge, but the majority of those Aaron knew would not. Especially not Mira, who would no doubt eagerly take over gathering donations.

Several minutes later, they arrived at Lacy's house. Aaron paused on the sidewalk, but she turned to him. "Do you want to come in? You haven't met my mother and sisters yet, and I'm sure my mother will want to thank you."

Aaron smiled. He looked forward to finally meeting her family. She led him inside the warm interior. Though Timothy had told him how sparsely furnished the house was, it still surprised him. How much had they sold to pay off their debt? Clearly anything that wasn't absolutely necessary for survival. They had nothing left in the way of decoration or sentimental value.

Lacy slipped off her coat and nodded to the pegs near the door. "You can hang your coat there."

Aaron did so as voices drifted from just down the hall. He had just retrieved his money pouch when a woman stepped into the entry.

"Lacy." She eyed them in surprise. "You're home early."

Lacy glanced at Aaron and then stepped forward. "Mother, this is Aaron."

Mrs. Evern's face lifted in a kind smile. "Aaron, how nice to finally meet you."

"You as well, Mrs. Evern."

She motioned him toward her and into the kitchen. "You can call me Helen."

Lacy's two sisters sat at the table, and their mother introduced them. Once Aaron had greeted them, attention turned to Lacy.

"Did Victor give you the evening off?" her mother asked.

Lacy shook her head. Aaron was afraid her panic would return, but she spoke calmly. "I told Aaron about the baby."

Helen looked at him, her expression sobering, but Lacy continued.

"He paid my debt to Victor so that I could quit. He is going to help take care of us."

Helen's mouth fell open. Her eyes turned teary. "You're keeping the baby?"

Lacy nodded, moisture filling her own eyes.

Helen turned to Aaron again, gratitude beaming from her face. "Thank you." She shook her head, seeming to grasp the full reality of the situation. "That is more than anyone should have to do."

Aaron merely smiled. "I am happy to do it." He set his money pouch on the table, the coins clanking. It was probably more than they had seen in a long time. "That should be enough to make your next payment to Banson. We can figure out what to do from there."

"You're too kind," Helen murmured, her tears just about to fall.

Aaron shrugged. He would always help those who struggled, but this was more than he would do for just anyone. He glanced at Lacy. She had to know that. So did her mother.

Setting that aside for now, Aaron eyed the bare kitchen cabinets. "I still have money left. I can get you some more food." With the baby coming, Lacy needed more than she was getting from her meager pay.

She appeared ready to protest, but her mother spoke first. "We would appreciate that very much."

She gave her daughter a look. Helen was probably thinking of the baby, the same as Aaron. Lacy still didn't look entirely comfortable with it.

"It's just temporary," Aaron said, hoping to reassure her. "If we can find you another way to make money, you can always pay me back eventually." He hastily added, "Not that it's necessary." He didn't want them to feel like they owed another debt.

Lacy let out a slow sigh. "All right."

Chances were they wouldn't find Lacy a new job, especially with her previous employment, but that could be dealt with another time. He was fully aware that, in taking her away from her job, he may be responsible for their wellbeing for the rest of his life.

"I'll head out to one of the shops now," he said. It was getting late. They would be sitting down to supper soon. It was probably best to let Lacy and her family talk through this sudden change anyway.

Back outside, he hurried to the merchants' row and bought what bread, vegetables, and meat he could afford—enough to last Lacy and her family for a couple of days. Aaron prayed spring would come quickly and hunting would get better. It would be far easier providing for them when he could hunt game on his own and gather wild edibles. Everything cost at least double this winter.

In less than an hour, he returned to the house with the food. Hannah and Gwen eyed it with obvious desire while Lacy and her mother thanked him profusely. They invited him to stay for supper, but he reluctantly declined. Timothy would wonder where he was, especially after practically flying in and out of the house earlier.

The walk back gave him time to consider how to explain this to his brother. It was more than a little reckless. He didn't try to deny that, but he didn't see that he had much choice. In another week or two, Victor would have found out about the baby, and Lacy would have ended the pregnancy.

When he arrived home, he shrugged off his coat and pried off his boots with a sigh, the weariness of the long day settling. A moment later, Timothy stepped into the entry.

"I was starting to think we should go out looking for you."

Aaron straightened. "Everything's fine." At least, that's what he prayed.

Timothy nodded into the kitchen. "Dillon has supper ready. We were just about to sit down."

Aaron followed him, and they each dished up a bowl of soup. As Timothy turned for the table where the other men were taking seats, Aaron stopped him.

"Let's eat in the living room. We need to talk."

Timothy glanced at the others but nodded. They left the kitchen and took seats across from each other next to the fireplace in the small living room. Timothy offered a prayer for the meal, and then all was quiet. Aaron stared at his soup, but the matters in his mind were more pressing than his appetite.

"I paid off Lacy's debt to Victor so she could quit working at the Briar. I'm going to take care of her and her family until we can figure things out. That includes making payments on their three hundred pound debt to Mr. Darwin."

Aaron watched Timothy digest this. As expected, uncertainty lurked in his expression.

"Are you sure you can do that?"

"I'll pick up as much work at the docks as I can." He'd made things work in Dunlow. He would do the same here. "I know how foolish it sounds, and maybe it is that foolish." He winced. "But I did it for a reason. Lacy is six months pregnant."

Timothy's eyes widened.

"No one knew but her family. She broke down and told me. She won't be able to keep it hidden for much longer, and Victor would have had her end it as soon as he found out."

Timothy nodded slowly now. "How is she taking it?"

"She was scared, but she seemed to be doing all right when I left."

"And she wants to keep the baby?"

Aaron nodded. It was rather remarkable, considering the circumstances. No doubt her mother's influence helped with that.

He sighed again. "I know what I've gotten myself into and that I probably rushed into it faster than I should have, but I just didn't want her to have to lose that baby."

AARON ACCEPTED HIS wages for the day and deposited the coins in his pocket. He cast a glance around to make sure no one was paying too much attention. Anyone could try to jump him once he left the docks. But everyone nearby appeared too busy to notice. It had been a good payday. He'd been able to earn extra by helping to repair one of the masts on a ship. Elôm willing, his ease with climbing and heights would be talked about, and he'd get even more work.

Today, however, the work was done, and he left the docks behind, taking the now familiar route to Lacy's house. He would give them most of the money while keeping just enough to put in his share for food and such back at home. He didn't mind that at all. In the week since Lacy had quit working at the Briar, her health already seemed drastically improved. The paleness was gone, and she'd filled out faster than Aaron would have expected. There was no hiding the baby now. He smiled. He was quite looking forward to meeting the little one. So were Ben and Mira. They'd talked of little else at the meeting two days ago.

Aaron rounded the corner to Lacy's street. A female yell sent icy chills streaking through him. Just ahead, a group of four men were gathered outside Lacy's house. Two of them dragged Helen between them.

"Let her go!"

Lacy grabbed at one of the men, while Gwen dove at the other. The man gave a backhanded swipe but just missed the younger girl. The other man, however, shrugged Lacy off and shoved her. She landed in a snow bank at his side. Hannah rushed to her.

Fury bursting through him, Aaron charged toward the fray. The men seemed confused by his arrival at first, which gave him an opening to act. He punched one of them full in the face and then shouldered the other away from Helen. The moment she was free, he looked for Lacy to make sure she was all right.

In that brief second, one of the other men rammed into him. Aaron stumbled but kept his feet. He pushed against the man and landed a blow to his stomach, but the others descended quickly. Despite his best efforts, their attacks landed much more swiftly and brutally than the ones he managed. After a savage blow to the gut, his legs buckled, and he landed in the hard packed snow. Even then, the attack continued, pummeling his head, stomach, and back. He tried to protect himself, but it did little good. Between the stunning blows, he heard Lacy screaming for them to stop.

At last, the attack ceased. Aaron gasped for breath, pain stabbing through his ribs and throbbing in his stomach. His head pounded and swirled, unconsciousness edging in. Ice and snow crunched nearby. Aaron held his eyes shut but fought to remain awake and focus on the harsh voice that echoed above him.

"You better have at least half of it next time, or one of you will be in the workhouses. And keep him from interfering unless you want him dead."

These words were spat with malice before the footsteps trudged off and were lost in the midst of gasping coughs.

"Hannah, take Mother inside. Gwen, help me."

Aaron's mind cleared further at the sound of Lacy's voice, and he forced his eyes open. She knelt in front of him, her own eyes rounded in fear.

"Aaron?"

He gritted his teeth and grimaced at the taste of blood. "I'm all right."

Not that he could be sure, but he didn't want her to worry. Chances were he had a broken rib or two and a concussion. His left side sure burned as if ribs were broken.

Lacy gripped his right arm, and Gwen took the other. They helped him sit up and then get to his feet. He groaned and struggled to stay upright as the ground tilted sharply. He drew in the deepest breath he could and let his head clear. Lacy and Gwen then guided him into the house.

In the kitchen, Helen sat in a chair, breathing from a vial. Her breaths were still ragged. Hannah stood next to her, a hand resting on her shoulder, though Aaron could only see them through one eye. The other was swelling shut.

Lacy and Gwen helped him ease down into a chair. Aaron grabbed Lacy's arm as she started to turn away.

"Are you all right?" He cleared his throat, blood clogging his voice. If she lost the baby because of the rough treatment from those men...

"I'm fine." Her voice was clipped. She turned and pulled out of his grasp. On the way to the fireplace, she instructed, "Gwen, get me some clean cloths."

Gwen rushed to do her bidding, and Lacy poured a steaming kettle of water into a basin. When Gwen set the cloths on the table next to it, she asked, "Should I go get his brother?"

Aaron held up his hand, biting back a groan at the pain it caused his ribs. "No, I'll be fine." Gwen shouldn't go out alone just to get Timothy.

Lacy was silent a moment before she finally said, "We'll wait for now. Just help me get him cleaned up."

She grabbed a cloth and pressed it to his lip. "Hold this to get the bleeding stopped."

Aaron reached up to hold the cloth and rested his elbow on the table. Lacy then pressed another cloth to his forehead above his swollen eye. She held it there for a couple of minutes. By now, Helen breathed easier, but Aaron's anger still simmered. What if the ordeal and the cold weather had killed her? Or what if Lacy or one of her sisters had been injured? His own breathing grew harder, paining his chest.

He pulled the cloth away from his lip. "What happened? Were those Darwin's men?"

Lacy looked him in the eye and appeared hesitant to speak. Even so, he was going to find out, one way or another. He didn't care what authority they had. They shouldn't be able to come and try to drag a woman away like that. Lacy must have read the determination in his expression. She relented, but everything about her face said she didn't want to.

"Yes, it was Banson and his men." She drew a breath as if to calm herself, but a very deep look of fear flashed in her eyes. "Mr. Darwin found out I quit working at the Briar." She paused again. She seemed to have trouble with the words. "He said he's getting impatient. He wants the debt paid. He wants at least half of it paid up right now."

Her voice trembled at the end.

Half? Where would they get that kind of money?

They'd just have to find a way.

"I'll talk to him," Aaron assured her, but this almost seemed to make her more upset, judging by the tight knit of her brow. He sensed that she might be angry with him, though he couldn't figure out why. Maybe she blamed him for this—for sticking his nose into their business. He winced.

"Sorry," she murmured.

But it had nothing to do with the pain from his injuries. Should he have just left them alone? *Was I wrong, Elôm?* He wrestled with this question for a moment but then thought of the baby. With the way she was showing, Victor would have had her get rid of it by now. He had to believe doing what he could to save that baby was the right thing.

Lacy pulled the cloth away from his forehead. She leaned closer to inspect the wound there, and Aaron tried not to enjoy her nearness too much.

"It has stopped bleeding," she said, "but it needs stitches." She set her bloodied cloth aside.

"Do we need to find a physician?" Gwen asked.

Aaron watched Lacy out of his one good eye. She bit her lip.

"Can you stitch it?" He didn't want Gwen going out

for a physician any more than he wanted her going out to get Timothy.

Lacy sighed, but then nodded. "Yes. I stitched up Victor once after he broke up a bar fight."

Looking resigned, she walked over to a cabinet and pulled out a small canvas bundle. She unrolled it on the table to reveal a sewing kit. After cleaning and threading a needle, she faced Aaron again.

"I'm not very experienced at this," she admitted. "If you want, we can still get a physician."

"I'm sure you'll do fine." Aaron gave her a small smile. She didn't return it, but at least she didn't look so upset anymore.

He sat still and gripped the side of the chair as she began stitching. The needle seemed a bit blunt, and he had to bite down hard not to groan, but it only took a couple of stitches for her to finish. She then wet a fresh cloth and cleaned his face.

"Your eye will probably be swollen for a few days. Do you think anything is broken?"

Aaron breathed out slowly, the stab in his ribs attempting to speak for him. "A couple of ribs, probably, but nothing serious that I can tell."

Lacy didn't look entirely comforted.

"I'll have someone check me over later," he assured her. One of their newer congregation members was just starting out as a physician.

Now that he was taken care of, a guarded and distant look returned to Lacy's face. Aaron wanted to ask her about it, but not in front of the rest of her family. Letting it go, he looked over at Helen.

"How are you doing?"

She gave him a weak smile. "Much better. It'll just take a little bit for my lungs to recover. I'll be all right."

Just so long as the same thing didn't happen again. Determination hardened inside of Aaron, fighting against the uncertainty that whispered in. He gripped the table and pushed to his feet. Dizziness threatened to sit him back down, but it passed quickly enough.

"I should get back home and talk to Timothy so we can figure out what to do about Darwin."

Lacy eyed him critically. "Are you sure you can make it?"

Aaron nodded, though it did nothing to help the splitting headache intensifying in his skull. He needed to rest and let his body heal, but Darwin wouldn't wait for anyone.

"Timothy or I will check in and make sure Banson and his men don't try something again."

After trading goodbyes with Lacy's family, Aaron walked out of the kitchen. Lacy followed him. When she grabbed her coat and slipped it on, he gave her a questioning look. He wasn't going to let her walk him home. She should take it easy after the stress of today.

But she brushed past him and opened the door.

"I need to talk to you," she said as she stepped outside.

Aaron followed. He had a feeling that the anger he sensed earlier was about to resurface, and his stomach churned a little. He wasn't sure what he'd say if she blamed him for this.

Standing out on the snowy path, Lacy held her coat tightly around herself and turned to him. Her face was set and almost steely, though her eyes watered. With deadly calm, she looked him in the eyes. "I'm going to ask Victor for my job back."

The declaration socked Aaron right in his already-throbbing gut. He drew a breath, but she cut him off before he could protest.

"If Mr. Darwin knows I'm working again, there's a chance I can convince him to let me keep paying off the debt in smaller amounts."

Aaron grimaced, his chest aching from more than his cracked ribs. "What about the baby?"

She cast her eyes down now and wouldn't look at him when she spoke. "I have no choice."

Aaron shook his head, desperation clawing in. If she did this, she would never be the same, and if she returned to working for Victor, it would likely be for the rest of her life. His tightening throat tried to strangle his voice. "Don't."

She lifted her eyes once more, the tears more evident now, but her voice came out hard. "I have to. If I don't, they'll drag my mother away, and she'll die. Then they'll come for one of us. How would my sisters take care of themselves if I'm taken to the workhouse next? They would end up just like me." A tear dripped from her flashing eyes. "I will *not* let that happen."

Aaron could understand that. He had felt the same way about keeping Timothy out of the mines. But the thought of her getting rid of the baby and returning to the Briar made him physically ill. For all he knew, she would do it the moment he left.

"Lacy." He wanted to reach out to her, but her rigid posture and closed off expression held him back. "Please, just let me talk to some of my friends. There's a chance I can get the money. I can talk to Mr. Darwin. I'll work every single day if I have to."

But she was already shaking her head before he even finished. "Didn't you hear what Banson said? He'll kill you if you don't stay out of this."

Fear joined the pain in her eyes.

"I'll be fine."

She scrunched up her face, her fists clenching. She speared him with as close to a glare as he had seen from her, exasperation in her voice. "Why are you doing this? Why are you even helping me? Why would you take this on yourself? No one does that."

Her eyes demanded the truth from him.

Aaron sighed. "Because I know what it's like to struggle to provide for your family. I know what it's like to trudge home from work exhausted, praying for something to get even a little bit better." He paused, his pounding heart adding to the throbbing in his chest. He should have just told her from the beginning. "And because I care about you."

Her shoulders drooped a little, though he couldn't tell whether it was disappointment or something else. "Aaron—"

This time he stopped her. "I know it's probably foolish of me, but I can't say your smile gave me much choice."

Despite the frown marring her face, that smile peeked out unbidden.

It drew one to his own swollen lips. "See, it gets me every time."

She ducked her head, trying to hide it. She stood that way for a moment before looking up again. They grew serious once more as Aaron continued.

"But, regardless of how I feel, all I want is to see you, the baby, your sisters, and your mother safe, healthy, and happy. Whatever happens or doesn't happen after that makes no difference. I just want to be your friend and don't want you to have to make decisions that might haunt you for the rest of your life. This might be hard to believe considering most of the men you've known, but I'm not looking to get anything from you. I simply want to help you." He held back a grimace. This was hard. "But, if you tell me right now to go and let you handle this, then, Elôm help me, I will."

Tears welled again as she battled the emotions in her expression. Her strength seemed to be abandoning her. Her chest heaved, and her voice broke, raw vulnerability taking over. "I want to tell you to go. I don't want to see you get hurt, but…I can't handle this by myself, and neither can my mother or sisters."

She hung her head and wrapped her arms tightly around her growing middle. Her next words broke out in a sob. "I don't want to lose my baby."

That did Aaron in.

He stepped forward and put his arms around her. She clung to his coat and cried against his chest. Heaven help him, he wanted to prevent her from ever having to cry again. She gathered herself together just a few moments later and pulled away. However, the lingering fear in her eyes still tore him up. He didn't know how, but he would find some way to make this better.

He rested his hands on her shoulders. "You know I have contact with Alex Avery. I'll go to him. Maybe he can help us get the money." He'd rather be indebted to Avery than a man like Darwin. At least Avery was fair and had a heart.

Lacy nodded, biting her lip.

"You don't have to lose your baby," Aaron told her softly.

She closed her eyes, tears still dribbling down her reddened cheeks. When she opened them again, she stared up at him. "I just don't want something to happen to you either. Banson is powerful and dangerous."

"I promise I'll be careful."

Though he hated to part with her, he let his hands slide from her shoulders. He needed to set things in motion before Banson made his next move.

"I'll let you know when I've talked to Avery."

She nodded, and he turned to go but hesitated. A heavy weight pressed down on him that he could not ignore, yet to put it into words was one of the hardest things he'd ever had to do. He faced her again. His own fear he'd kept buried, but it rushed up now in a breath-snatching wave of doubt. Everything he was doing could crash down around them with devastating consequences. He wanted to force the truth away, deep down where it wouldn't touch him until after this was over, but that wasn't fair to Lacy.

He looked her in the eyes. "I can't promise I can fix this." He gritted his teeth. She had placed her life, her baby's, and her family's lives in his hands—both when she'd left the tavern with him and today—but what assurance did he possibly have to offer her? "Elôm knows I'll do everything in my power to protect you, but I just pray you won't hate me in the end because of my interference."

He walked on then, the burden only growing heavier.

What if he had acted rashly and Lacy and her family reaped the consequences? Had he stepped in where he shouldn't have? *Elôm, if I've erred, let me, not them, suffer for it.*

"Aaron."

He stopped and looked over his shoulder. Lacy still stood where she was, her cheeks yet damp.

"Thank you for getting me away from the tavern." She rubbed her nose and appeared to fight back more tears. "I didn't think anyone but my family would ever care about me again."

AARON CLOSED THE door quietly, but Timothy must have heard it anyway. His brother stepped into the entry before he had time to turn his swollen face away and explain.

"What happened?"

Aaron winced. "That debt collector, Banson, tried to drag Helen off to the workhouse. He must have decided to leave it alone for now after I stepped in."

"Are they all right?"

"At the moment."

Aaron unbuttoned his coat and struggled to slip it off. Timothy rushed up to help him.

"Do you need me to get Rodin?"

"Later." Aaron wrapped his arm around his chest. Rodin wouldn't be able to do much more than give him a painkiller anyway. Broken ribs would just have to heal themselves in time. "I have things I need to figure out first."

He trudged into the living room and sank down on the sofa. He shouldn't sit down—not with his body stiffening up as it was—but he needed to catch his breath after the walk home. Timothy sat on the edge of the short table in front of him, and Aaron explained what had happened. When he finished, Timothy rubbed his forehead and appeared just as uncertain of what to do as Aaron was.

"Banson will come back again for the money. Soon." Aaron held his ribs and sighed heavily. "I can't let him take one of them away."

Timothy sat in silence for a long time. At last, he said, "What about Landale? They'd be safe in camp for now."

If only it were that simple. "I thought of that, but Helen could never travel there in the cold. She wouldn't be able to leave until it warmed up—another three months at least. And Lacy would never leave her."

Whatever they did, they didn't have that long to wait. At this point, he could see only one solution, though there were no guarantees.

"I need to see Avery. Tonight." Aaron sat forward, shoving aside the aches and pains of protest from his body.

Timothy cast him a skeptical look. "I don't think you're in any condition to be heading out across the city again."

"I don't have much choice."

Aaron pushed to his feet. Pressure rushed into his head, increasing the steady throbbing. He closed his eyes and let it subside. He then heard Timothy sigh, but his brother didn't try to change his mind. Instead, he walked with Aaron back to the entry and grabbed his coat.

"I'll go with you. You might not make it back by yourself."

Aaron nodded to him in thanks. He didn't want to admit Timothy might be right. But he'd let his body rest once this was taken care of.

Outside, twilight was taking hold as they set off in silence. Aaron took these moments to pray for Lacy and for a good outcome with Avery. He also prayed desperately for wisdom. If things didn't work out tonight, he would need a plan, fast.

He darted glances at the streets they passed. He didn't like having only one good eye. It made him feel less perceptive. But Timothy knew the dangers. He'd keep a lookout where Aaron couldn't. Elôm willing, they wouldn't come across any trouble. Aaron had seen enough of it today.

"We'll try the Red Crane," he said after several blocks.

He and Timothy didn't speak along the way. He couldn't help wondering what his brother thought of all this. Did he disapprove of the entire thing? The thought made him uncomfortable. Still, even if Timothy had his reservations, Aaron had no doubt his brother would support him through it. They could always count on each other that way.

By the time they arrived at the well-established tavern, Aaron's ribs screamed and the exertion made him light-headed. He refused to let it overwhelm him as he stepped into the tavern. He scanned the tables. Thank Elôm. Avery sat right at a table near the fireplace with Tavor and a couple of other men. Aaron eyed the empty seat on the opposite side of the table. At least if he reached it, he wouldn't have to worry about collapsing in front of everyone.

He set out across the room, skirting the other occupied tables. Avery spotted him quickly. At least now that they were acquainted, neither Avery nor Tavor gave him looks of suspicion. Avery actually appeared pleased to see him, though questions formed in his eyes.

"Looks like you had your hands full," Avery said when they reached the table. "I hope the other guy looks worse."

"Unfortunately, no." Aaron pulled out the chair and sat down, biting back the groan pushing up through his chest. "I need your help."

"All right," Avery responded slowly.

The last time they'd come to him for help, things hadn't gone so smoothly. Aaron glanced up at Timothy, who stood beside him. Though his brother rarely joined him in such places, Timothy appeared calm and collected. Aaron had no doubt he was praying this very minute. With a prayer of his own, he faced Avery.

"I'm sure you heard what I did for Lacy."

Avery made a point of knowing what went on in the taverns that he used to conduct his business.

"I did. I'd ask why the sudden need to get her out, but rumor has it, she's with child."

Aaron nodded. "She is."

"It's not yours, is it?"

Aaron gave him the coldest look he could manage, beat up as he was.

Avery raised his hand. "Forget I asked. People do talk though, considering how much time you spend at the Briar."

"That's the least of my concerns right now." However, he supposed he should address it at some point, especially if such talk spread to their congregation.

"So what exactly is it you need from me?"

"Lacy's family owes a large debt to Mr. Darwin. His debt collector tried to drag Mrs. Evern off to the workhouse today."

Avery gave him a perceptive look. "And you intervened."

Aaron nodded slowly.

"How large a debt are we talking?"

"Three hundred pounds."

Avery raised his brows. "If you're going to ask to borrow money, I'm afraid I won't be of much help. You know I deal in commodities, and what you and your friends paid me for the remedy has already been spent on food and supplies."

Aaron let out his breath slowly. He had hoped Avery would have some to spare. "If there is anything I could borrow from you, I'd appreciate it, but what I could really use are some extra sets of eyes to keep watch on Lacy and her family. I don't know when that debt collector will show up again. In exchange, if you need an extra man for something that doesn't involve stealing or killing, I can help out."

Avery thought it over for a moment before offering a nod. "I suppose I can spare a few men to keep an eye on things."

"Thank you." Aaron glanced at Tavor and the other two men who were high-ranking members of Avery's group. "It's just Lacy, her mother, and sisters, so if you would keep that in mind in choosing the men, I'd be grateful."

"I'll hand pick them myself."

Aaron gave him a few more brief specifics and then prepared to leave. He had to lean heavily on the table to get to his feet. Walking home wouldn't be fun. Gritting his teeth, he straightened and pressed his hand to his ribs. Before he could turn to go, Avery spoke again.

"I'll see what I can get together as far as funds. It won't be free, but I trust you're good for it."

"Thank you."

He then led the way out of the tavern. However, when they reached the street, Timothy stepped up beside him, took his arm on his less bruised side, and put it around his shoulders. Aaron hated to look so vulnerable out in the open like this, but he couldn't say he wasn't grateful for his brother's support. His strength was abandoning him faster than he could fight it.

Commotion came from the kitchen where the others must be working on supper when they arrived back at the house. Timothy helped Aaron slip his coat and boots off and then guided him into the living room. Aaron sank carefully down onto the sofa. This time he probably wouldn't get back up for a long while.

"I'll take one of the others and get Rodin," Timothy told him.

Aaron simply nodded. He didn't think he needed another examination, but it would probably make Timothy feel better.

When his brother walked out of the room, Aaron rested back against the cushions and closed his eyes. Quiet enveloped him for a few minutes before the others from the kitchen came to check on him.

"You look like you had a mine fall on you." Dillon and his brother were from the Graylin Valley same as Aaron and Timothy. The four shared a lot in common.

Aaron snorted out a harsh laugh. "That's about what it feels like."

He briefly rehashed what had happened, and they brought him supper. Timothy returned a short time later with their physician. As Aaron suspected, he had a couple of cracked ribs and a concussion. Rodin ordered him to take it easy and rest for a few days. Aaron received the instructions quietly. He wasn't sure there would be much resting until Lacy and her family didn't have to worry about Darwin anymore.

Later on, when the other men were busy cleaning up the kitchen, Timothy entered the living room and handed Aaron a chunk of ice wrapped in a dishcloth. Aaron pressed it against his swollen eye and looked at his brother with the other.

"I'm an idiot, aren't I, for getting myself into this?"

Timothy sat down across from him and didn't answer immediately. "They needed help."

Yes, but that didn't change how he'd gone about it. "Do you think I acted foolishly in taking Lacy away from the tavern before figuring things out first?"

Timothy thought about this for another moment. "Maybe, but...I know you did what you thought was right. There wasn't much time with the baby."

Aaron let out a long sigh. "I didn't give it much prayer first. I wanted to get Lacy out and that was my opportunity so I took it. Now I'm afraid I've only made things worse for them and won't be able to fix it."

"Well, it's never too late for dedicated prayer. And remember, Elôm cares about them even more than you do."

AARON GROANED AS he rolled over. He'd suffered broken ribs once before. He, Timothy, and Josan had nearly starved in the weeks he couldn't work. Thank Elôm those days were over. He grimaced. Except now he just had other things—other people—to be concerned about.

He pushed himself up, gripping his ribs to try to hold back the pain. Letting his feet rest on the floor, he just sat on the edge of the bed. He hadn't spent enough time in quiet prayer the last couple of weeks. That would change now.

He bowed his head. "I've made a mess of things, Lord."

He'd been so concerned about Lacy that he hadn't consulted Elôm before he'd acted. Concern was no excuse for that. Even in the last week, he'd spent so much more time focusing on what he had to do to provide for Lacy and her family that he hadn't asked Elôm what he should do. He confessed all of this and earnestly sought Elôm's guidance for his next move. He prayed for wisdom, clear direction, and the patience and trust to wait on Elôm's answers instead of charging ahead. He was too used to seeing needs and addressing them one way or another. Their difficult life in Dunlow had taught him this, but he could see now his failures to wait and rest in Elôm even then. He was a man of action. Sometimes that was good and had helped them survive, but just as often it threatened to interfere with his faith.

After a long time of giving his different scenarios, plans, and questions to Elôm, he finally stood up. His body dragged and pained him, but his heart felt lighter even with the uncertainties that still hovered. Aaron dressed slowly and headed downstairs. The smell of breakfast greeted him halfway down. Only now did he realize that he'd slept in longer than normal. Usually he was up with the sun and down at the docks waiting for work. How would he work now? He shook his head. There he went, already worrying about what he could or couldn't do.

When he stepped into the kitchen, he found Timothy sitting at the table with Ben. The older man winced when he looked up at him. A quick glimpse in the mirror before he'd left his room had told Aaron that his still-swollen eye and jaw sported ugly bruises.

Before Ben could speak, Timothy gestured to a chair. "I'll get you breakfast."

Aaron eased himself down in the chair facing Ben while Timothy dished him a plate of food.

"I heard what happened," Ben said.

"Well, I probably had it coming and brought it on myself."

Ben raised his brows, and Aaron explained, "I haven't been very patient in letting Elôm work these days."

Ben nodded slowly. "Unfortunately, we sometimes need reminders of our own inability to control the world around us."

Aaron let out a short laugh. Wasn't that the truth? He then released a long sigh and rubbed his ribs. "Looks like I'll be out of work for a bit, which means there will be nothing coming in for Lacy and her family. I'm praying Elôm will give me clear direction because I'm at a loss. Darwin won't wait around for that money, and unless we somehow come up with one-hundred fifty pounds, we'll have no way to hold him off."

"You know I'll give you as much as I can. We can ask the others, but…"

Ben had no need to finish. Everyone had already given everything they could to purchase the remedy last month.

"Still, we can ask," Ben said more hopefully. "Elôm will provide."

Aaron gave a nod, forcing himself to hold onto those words. Since when had trust become so much more difficult?

Probably when his heart had become so deeply involved in the situation.

Shortly after Ben left and Aaron had eaten his breakfast, he pushed up from the table. Rodin would tell him to rest for the day, but, as long as he didn't overdo it, he wasn't just going to sit around. He needed to see how Lacy was doing today. Though she had changed her mind about returning to her job, he was still afraid she might panic and do it anyway. He'd had trouble sleeping last night as he'd contemplated discovering she had gotten rid of the baby. Even though it wasn't his, something inside him grew ill at the thought.

That wondering and ache in his stomach drove him now. He stepped into the entry and bent over for his boots. Though it took longer than it should have, he managed to get them on. It left him out of breath, however, and he paused before reaching for his coat.

"Let me help you."

Timothy walked in and set his usual leather satchel down. He helped Aaron slip his coat on before reaching for his own.

"Heading to the warehouse?" Aaron asked.

Timothy shook his head. "I'm going with you. I thought I'd start a study of the Scrolls with Lacy and her family. They seemed very interested when I mentioned it. At least Hannah and Gwen did."

Aaron smiled. That was the best news he'd had all morning. And it would look less questionable to have Timothy there with him to anyone who was paying attention and prone to talk.

When they arrived, Aaron scanned the street and spotted one of Avery's men watching the house from an inconspicuous location. He gave Aaron a brief nod, and Aaron dipped his head in response. While it didn't solve their problems, it helped to know he had someone keeping an eye on things when he couldn't.

Timothy knocked on the door. A moment later, it opened, and Lacy peeked out. As soon as she saw it was them, she swung the door open wider. Aaron studied her face. She appeared calm and rested—a bit of a miracle after yesterday.

"Come in," she invited.

They stepped inside. After they had removed their coats, she led them into the kitchen, where they greeted the others.

"I brought more passages from the King's Scrolls," Timothy said, setting his satchel on the table. "I thought, if you were not busy this morning, you might be interested in starting a study with me."

Helen smiled warmly. "That's very kind of you. Why don't you sit down and I'll make us some tea."

While Timothy took a seat and quickly struck up a conversation with Hannah and Gwen, Aaron turned to Lacy.

"I spoke to Alex Avery last night."

Her expression pulled a little tighter in seriousness as she focused her full attention on him.

"I asked him if he could spare some men to keep an eye on things here, in case Banson shows up again when I'm not around."

"He's willing to do that?"

"In exchange I offered to give him a hand sometimes when he needs an extra man. He has someone outside right now."

Lacy breathed slowly in and out as if not sure what to make of it. Finally, she nodded. "I guess that will make us feel better."

Aaron gave her a half smile. "I'd do it myself, but unfortunately, even my crete blood doesn't give me the ability stay up twenty-four hours a day."

A smile bloomed on her face—soft and grateful—and his heart thumped his bruised ribs. Though the smile slowly waned, she held his gaze for a long moment.

Finally, she pulled her eyes away and motioned to the chair in front of him. "Have a seat."

Aaron did as commanded but continued to watch her. Her cheek twitched as if another smile threatened as she turned away from him to help her mother. He let his gaze linger a moment longer before he shifted his attention to the conversation at the table. Timothy was answering questions Gwen and Hannah had about some of the letters he'd given them last time. Their enthusiasm encouraged Aaron, and he prayed they would pass it on to Lacy.

A few minutes later, she came to his side again and set a cup of tea in front of him.

"Thank you." He slid the steaming cup a little closer and reached for the sugar dish.

He paused at Lacy's quiet voice. "You look awful, by the way."

Aaron looked up to see her grinning. The teasing glint in her eyes was delightful.

"Thanks. You look lovely."

The pink blush that spread across her cheeks made her even more so. She rested her hand on her stomach. "Well, at the rate I'm growing now, that might not be for much longer."

Aaron glanced at her filled-out figure. "Oh, I don't know, I think it's rather becoming."

Her blush deepened to a rosy red, and he couldn't help but smile. However, it died when she turned away. The calmness that allowed her to tease him rested on one thing—her trust that he would take care of them. He'd asked her to trust him, but now he had no idea if he could make good on it. What if he led her family into more pain than they'd had to face before he'd intervened? The thought of causing her pain stabbed him right in the heart with a force that hurt worse than cracked ribs. He winced and then noticed Lacy watching him, her brow knit. He smoothed his own face and offered a smile. Hopefully, she would just think it was from his injuries and not uncertainty over the future.

Lacy and her mother joined them at the table for the study. Aaron forced himself to focus on his brother's words. Thinking on and learning more of Elôm was a far sight better than letting his fears take over yet again.

Timothy's quiet though strong voice filled the small kitchen. It wasn't commanding, yet it drew listeners in. Aaron had witnessed this at their meetings and again now around the table. Despite the lack of formal learning, he had become a gifted teacher. Aaron smiled to himself as he thought of the groups of children and women Timothy used to teach to read back in Dunlow. He'd loved that, but this was his true calling.

Eventually, they moved into the living room where they had more comfortable seating. During the study, Lacy's sisters listened attentively, and Gwen had many eager questions for Timothy. Their mother seemed to listen closely as well as she worked on sewing what Aaron eventually realized was an infant-sized shirt. The sight of it warmed him inside, yet the glow died when he glanced at Lacy. Something about her expression looked troubled, perhaps with discomfort. She stared down at her lap and tugged at the ragged edges of her sleeves, never saying a word or even looking up when her sisters spoke. Even her cup of tea sat untouched, the steam curling above it gradually disappearing as it grew cold.

The morning passed by, and despite Lacy's apparent discomfort, Aaron found the hours enjoyable. Sitting around with Timothy and the women gave him a feeling of home and family, something he hadn't experienced since leaving camp. Not that they didn't get along with Dillon and the others, but a group of bachelors just wasn't the same. And none of them could make up for lack of female company.

As lunchtime neared, Timothy started packing his things back into his satchel while still conversing with Hannah and Gwen.

"Can you come back tomorrow?" Gwen's eyes sparkled eagerly.

Timothy smiled at her enthusiasm. "I would, but we have a meeting tomorrow night that I'll be busy preparing for." He glanced at Aaron. "But, if you would like to join us, I know Aaron would be happy to walk you there."

Gwen looked at her mother.

"You're quite old enough to make such a decision yourself now," Helen encouraged her. "Go if you wish."

"I think I would like to," Gwen decided. "I want to see what it's like."

Hannah quickly agreed, and Aaron smiled. If those two were going, Lacy probably would too. She remained silent, her expression a bit taut. As if wanting to escape, she suddenly rose and grabbed her full teacup and Aaron's empty one and stepped out of the room. No one seemed to notice except for her mother.

Aaron traded a quick look with Helen and then pushed up from his chair. After sitting for so long, his body had stiffened up, and he winced as he straightened. He walked after Lacy. At the kitchen door, he paused and leaned against the doorframe. Lacy moved about as if trying to find anything to do to appear busy.

"Is something bothering you?"

She glanced at him. "I'm fine."

A flash of a forced smile said otherwise. Aaron continued to watch her. She must have felt his gaze because she looked up again.

"I'm tired." She shrugged. "It's getting harder to sleep comfortably at night."

Aaron wasn't sure that was the entirety it. After all, she had been smiling and teasing him before the study. But he wouldn't press her.

"Will you come to the meeting tomorrow night?"

She remained silent for a long moment, and Aaron studied her profile as she wiped the table. Her brows lowered, partially hidden by loose strands of hair.

"I suppose, if my sisters are going."

She didn't have nearly the same enthusiasm as Gwen, but Aaron would take it.

"I'll stop by for the three of you tomorrow evening then."

LACY SHOVED ASIDE one dress and then another. She frowned hard and blew out a sigh, but Gwen was too busy chattering at Hannah to notice. What in Ilyon would she wear to the meeting tonight? She rested her hand over her rapidly growing middle. Almost nothing fit her anymore, and she and her mother weren't done with any of her new dresses. Even if they had been finished, they were dreadfully plain and nothing more than altered hand-me-downs. The only new dresses she'd had in years were the ones Victor had given her for work. She winced and closed her eyes. Whatever she chose to wear tonight, leaving the past behind wasn't as easy or simple as leaving behind those dresses at the tavern. She couldn't just change out of that lifestyle and not expect it to affect the future. What would the people at the meeting think of her?

She clutched her stomach more tightly as fear swirled up inside of her. This was Aaron's world, not hers. She did not belong in it. What if she embarrassed him or tainted him somehow? He would probably hate her. That shouldn't matter as much as it did.

"Are you all right?"

Lacy straightened at Gwen's question and cast her sister a brief smile. "Yes."

No.

She should never have agreed to this. However, though she trusted Aaron more than any man since her father, something wouldn't let her watch Hannah and Gwen go alone. The city held so many dangers that one didn't even want to set foot outside. Of course, she wouldn't be able to do a single thing if they did meet trouble. After all, Aaron had been beaten right outside this house. Still, she had to accompany them for her own peace of mind.

She stiffened her spine. She could do this. Choosing the best dress she had available, she changed into it, and Hannah helped her tighten the lacing in the back. There was only just enough fabric to come together in the middle, and not nearly enough to remotely hide her swollen belly. Her condition would stick out clearly for all to see.

Outside their window, the sky grew dim. Aaron would show up any time now. Battling for strength, Lacy followed her sisters downstairs where their mother was putting away the last of their supper dishes. She smiled at Gwen and Hannah. When her attention reached Lacy, her eyes deepened with sympathy. She understood.

Only a moment later, a knock came at the door. She stepped into the hall to answer it. Both Aaron and Timothy stood outside. Lacy invited them in as her mother and sisters joined them. They greeted each other happily, and it was nice to see. They'd had little in the way of guests or friends since her father had died, but especially since she had started working for Victor. Though she had been prepared to live with that, she didn't want it for her sisters. They deserved a more normal life even if people would always shun her for the desperate choices she'd made to keep them from starving or dying in a workhouse.

She caught Aaron's eyes. His expression softened and took on a look of concern. Even beat up as he was, Lacy had to admit he was handsome. She'd always thought so, though she never let such thoughts go far. Daydreams of true love and happily-ever-after belonged to girls like Hannah and Gwen—young women who were innocent and unstained by the world's filth, something she would never again be able to claim.

Aaron's non-swollen eye narrowed slightly as if trying to read her thoughts. She forced a smile to her lips. Though he didn't seem convinced by it, he said nothing more than a deep, yet gentle, "Good evening."

She echoed him, fighting to keep her emotions in check. She had never met anyone so strong and capable yet bearing the ability for such gentleness. It was a hard combination to resist, particularly when combined with such honor. Goodness knew how it awakened the longing to share the rest of her life with such a man, but she had sacrificed those dreams for the survival of her family. She mustn't let herself forget it.

"Are you ready to go?" Aaron asked. He glanced at Hannah and Gwen.

The girls said yes and traded quick goodbyes with their mother.

"We won't be too late," Aaron assured her with a charming half smile.

Lacy's mother smiled in return, and Lacy could see

how much her mother liked him. That made it even more difficult. If only he could have shown up three years earlier.

Trooping outside, Timothy took the lead. Hannah and Gwen walked on either side of him. Lacy followed a couple of paces behind, and Aaron dropped back with her. They said nothing for a couple of minutes as they listened to Gwen ask an abundance of questions.

Finally, Lacy glanced up at Aaron. "I hope Timothy doesn't mind so many questions. None of us know what it's like to have a brother."

Aaron's smile grew again, full force this time. "Don't worry, he enjoys it. He has always loved to teach and is very passionate about what he does."

"How did he get to be so knowledgeable? Did he go to any school?"

"No, but our father and uncle spent a lot of time teaching him. The rest he learned for himself. He's always had a gift for sharing his knowledge."

"You must be very proud of him."

"Yes." The smile he sent Timothy's way would probably inspire just about anyone to do their best in life.

Lacy let a silent sigh slip past her lips. If only she had been born a man like Aaron. She could have done so much more for her family. Now she pulled in a deep breath of the cold air to steel herself. What was done was done. She couldn't change the past or its consequences. She merely had to live with them.

As they neared the warehouses down at the docks, Lacy's stomach turned, but it wasn't the morning sickness that still assaulted her sometimes. Her heart thumped too.

Shortly, they approached a large warehouse with boarded up windows. It wasn't much to look at and didn't even appear inhabited. However, the thinnest sliver of light glowed through a crack in the door. Of course, such a nondescript building was needed for such a gathering. If the queen knew it existed, they would all be executed.

Lacy halted as Timothy opened the door and let her sisters inside. Nausea rushed in so violently she had to swallow hard to keep her supper from coming up. They could all die for this. What was she letting her sisters get into? She gripped her stomach. If she died, so did the baby.

She jumped at a touch to her back.

"Easy," Aaron murmured. "Are you all right?"

Lacy looked up at him and released a quick breath. His hand pressed reassuringly to her back as his eyes searched hers. She breathed deeply, willing away the nauseous swirling of fear. Her sisters needed more than she or even their mother could provide. They needed friends and encouragement and hope. They could probably find all of that here. Despite the danger, she had to let them seek it. It might be the only thing that kept them from sinking into a life like her own if she couldn't keep things together.

She gave Aaron a tight nod and stepped resolutely to the door that Timothy held open for them.

Inside, the air was warmer than the outdoors, though it had no fireplace. Murmurs hummed through the open building, rising up from several groups that totaled around seventy people of varying ages. Lacy peered at them, her tongue growing thick and dry in her mouth. If only she could be invisible.

A lovely older woman broke from the crowd, followed shortly by a man around the same age. Lacy tensed as the couple walked straight toward them, but the woman's glowing smile calmed her. When the couple neared, Aaron drew Lacy forward and introduced her and her sisters.

"This is Mira and Ben," he told them.

So this was the couple Aaron had spoken of in the past. The same couple who had invited her and her family to their home on multiple occasions. Guilt jabbed a needle into her chest for never accepting their invitations, but they were so fine and proper. How could she have entered their home, especially while still working at the tavern?

"It's so good to finally meet you." Mira's lovely smile lit up her entire face, and she took Lacy's hands in her own. "You're even prettier than Aaron said you were."

Lacy couldn't help but smile, calmed by the woman's kind and motherly manner. She glanced at Aaron. He had his head ducked as if bashful. Was he blushing? Her smile grew a little wider.

"So are your sisters," Mira said as she greeted the two younger girls.

It was certainly a warmer welcome than Lacy had expected, yet no one else came forward to meet them.

After exchanging their greetings, Aaron led Lacy and her sisters deeper into the warehouse where everyone took seats amongst the lines of mismatched benches and chairs. He motioned to a few empty seats near the front. Lacy swallowed hard as Hannah and Gwen sat down. Everyone would be able to see her up here. She should have thought to ask to sit in the back, but it was too late now. Getting Hannah and Gwen up to move would be too obvious. She sat down slowly, and Aaron sat next to her. Ben and Mira sat just on the other side of her sisters. She tried to draw comfort from this, but it failed to bloom.

Murmurs and whispers came from all around her. Of course, the people could be talking about anything. It didn't mean it was about her. She chanced a glance around and caught eyes with an older woman across the aisle. Disapproval was written all over her pinched face, and she turned to whisper something to the woman next to her. Lacy quickly set her gaze straight ahead. So they were watching and talking about her. At least some of them. Her neck and cheeks grew hot and prickly.

Something brushed her hand, and Aaron gave it a quick squeeze. She looked over at him, and he offered her an encouraging smile before releasing her hand again. Her heart pattered, yet she felt no better. If anyone saw, it would only fuel the whispers. She set her hands firmly in her lap, clenching them as her palms grew sticky.

Timothy stepped to the front of the group a moment later, and the murmurs hushed. He greeted everyone and then called for them to bow their heads in prayer. Lacy tipped hers down in imitation but stared at her lap. The muscles in her back and shoulders squeezed with tension. What an impostor she was, sitting here like this. Her stomach roiled again.

Momentary relief washed through her when Timothy said "amen," though it was fleeting. As he began his teaching, Lacy tried to listen but felt as though eyes were burning into the back of her skull. She didn't dare look around to see if it was true, though she couldn't shake the feeling. Moisture built up along her back, making her dress cling to her skin. She clasped her hands tightly to keep from reaching back and rubbing away the discomfort. She might as well be on a pedestal in front of everyone. Any move she made would be noticed. She was sure of it.

After a while, her lower back ached from sitting in the hard chair, yet she didn't dare try shift into a more comfortable position. She wrapped her arms over her belly. Could the baby feel her unease? She closed her eyes in a desperate attempt to block out her surroundings. She wanted to go home. She wanted to hide.

At last, Timothy ended his message with another prayer. It was all Lacy could do not to jump up and flee the building. Not that she could actually jump in her condition. More like push herself up slowly and sigh at the chance to finally stretch her aching back.

Yet now she had to face all those piercing, disapproving eyes that likely saw her as a stain on their congregation. She kept her gaze cast down as Aaron led her toward the side of the building with Ben and Mira.

"Did you like the service?" Mira asked when they stopped.

Lacy looked up, forcing a smile to her lips. "Yes."

Liar. Honestly, she had heard almost nothing Timothy had said.

Mira's expression softened, as if she knew this. "It must be difficult for you to sit so long."

"A little." Better to have her think it was only physical discomfort than how much she hated being here amongst these people.

"Next time, I'll bring a cushion for you."

Lacy only smiled at the kind offer. There would not be a next time. She could not do this again.

Aaron touched her back lightly as he stepped to her side. "I have a few people I need to talk to. I'll be right back."

Lacy barely kept herself from stopping him as he stepped away. She didn't want to be left on her own. Even now, she felt the eyes, and when she looked around, it confirmed her suspicions. People *were* staring at her. Emotion welled up, constricting her throat, but she swallowed it down. These people had no right to judge her. They didn't even know her.

She lifted her chin slightly. This was her life, and she had to own it. While she wasn't proud of it, she had done what she had to in order to keep her family alive. She had a hard time believing these people, with their disapproving looks, wouldn't take drastic actions if their families were in danger of starving or being worked to death in a work-house. They might not understand her choices, but she did, and whatever that meant for the future, she would accept it.

Aaron crossed the warehouse to where a group of older gentlemen were speaking. The man at the center of the group, Matthias, was a successful merchant and one of the wealthiest members of their congregation besides Ben. Aaron hadn't been able to work since his confrontation with Banson, yet each day brought them closer to another visit from the debt collector. They weren't anywhere close to having the money they needed, and Aaron felt the direness of it weighing heavily.

He greeted the men in the group when they noticed him coming, and then focused on Matthias. "I need to talk to you about money. I know you gave a lot to get the remedy, but I was hoping I could borrow—"

"She's the prostitute?"

Aaron snapped his mouth shut. Matthias wasn't even looking at him. He followed the man's gaze over his shoulder to Lacy. He ground his teeth together and turned to face him again. "Her *name* is Lacy. And she's not anymore."

The man eyed Lacy for another moment before setting his gaze squarely on Aaron. "Is the child yours?"

Heat flushed through Aaron's veins. He would never have expected such a direct and insulting question. Not here.

"No, it's not mine. That's not why I visited the tavern. Whatever rumors are going around about it are not true." He paused and fought to temper his irritation. After all, he'd known full well the position he'd put himself in and what it looked like.

"What is true is that there's a pregnant woman and her family who are in dire need of help. I think we should all know by now that, regardless of where she came from or what situation she finds herself in, Elôm cares about her and would not have us turn our backs on someone in need. She is trying to turn her life around and shouldn't be condemned for her past. There are plenty of us who have faced the same thing."

He drew a breath to further calm himself before continuing. "If I can't raise enough money soon to appease the debt collector that is harassing them, then Lacy's mother, who has a very serious lung condition, will be hauled off to one of the workhouses. I came to ask you, and anyone else who's willing, for your help."

The man's lips thinned, and he shook his head. "I'm sorry, but I will not associate myself with a woman of her nature."

Aaron clenched his fists. "She was in a desperate situation. She didn't make the choice lightly."

But Matthias just shook his head again. "I'm sorry."

With that, he turned and walked away. Aaron looked imploringly at the others, but they only offered apologetic looks.

Releasing a long sigh, Aaron let his head and shoulders slump. Without Matthias and the others, he could never raise enough money here. It had been his last hope. Now how would he hold off Banson? He pressed his fingers to his forehead, the situation giving him a headache. *I don't know what to do, Lord. Show me a way, please.*

He raised his head and straightened. He wouldn't give up. He had to believe Elôm would guide him to a solution. Turning, he found Lacy where he'd left her, still standing with Mira. Hannah stood nearby, though Gwen had joined a group of other young women her age. They all giggled, and it brought a smile to his face. Gwen could probably charm her way into any group. Maybe he should have brought her to speak to Matthias. He'd like to see the man refuse her.

His gaze shifted back to Lacy. She didn't look nearly as comfortable here as Gwen did. The wide berth everyone but Ben and Mira gave her was painfully obvious. Tension coiled inside Aaron again. He had half a mind to call everyone to attention and demand to know if they really thought they were honoring Elôm with their behavior. However, it would probably mortify Lacy since she would be at the center of it all.

Swallowing down his disgust, he rejoined her. "Are you ready to go home?"

She looked up, her eyes wide and pleading, as though he'd just thrown her a lifeline. "Yes, please."

She did look exhausted. If he'd known she was so uncomfortable during the service, he would have offered his coat as a cushion for her to sit on. He could have kicked himself for not thinking of it.

"I'll get Gwen," he told her.

Once the girl had bid her new friends goodbye, Aaron led all three of them toward the door. Timothy gave him a nod from across the room when he noticed them. He would be here a while yet to speak with everyone, but Aaron wouldn't make Lacy wait through that.

Outside, the nearly full moons lit up the streets. Lacy pulled her coat more tightly around herself. When she finished arranging it, Aaron offered her his arm.

She hesitated a moment before wrapping her hand around it. They started off, Gwen and Hannah walking side by side just behind them. They had plenty to talk about, but their words were lost in Aaron's awareness of Lacy and what he could do to keep her safe. Neither of them said a word until they reached the girls' home. Aaron stepped inside with them just long enough to see Helen and tell them all goodnight. He lingered a moment as he stared at Lacy. He almost felt as though he should apologize for taking her to the meeting tonight, but a quiet goodbye was all they shared before he left.

Back at home, Aaron sat at the fireplace, mulling over his options, or rather, the lack thereof. He prayed for wisdom and answers and protection for Lacy's family. Sometime later, Timothy returned. As the other men went off to their rooms or into the kitchen, Timothy joined Aaron in the living room. He claimed a chair next to him, and they were quiet for a couple of minutes before Timothy finally spoke.

"There's a lot of talk."

Aaron glanced at him but said nothing.

"I'm afraid quite a few are questioning whether or not your interactions with Lacy have been entirely pure. They don't understand your dedication to helping her unless," Timothy cast him a somber look, "the baby is yours."

Aaron's neck prickled, and his muscles tensed. One or two people questioning his motives was one thing, but if a large part of their congregation was starting to doubt his integrity, it wasn't as easily dismissed.

"Do you believe me?" Aaron stared at his brother.

"Yes," Timothy answered, and Aaron didn't detect any doubt. "But me saying it isn't going to change what everyone is thinking."

Aaron nodded slowly. "What do you think I should do?"

Timothy gave it a moment of thought. "Many would probably tell you to back off a bit. To do what you can to help Lacy and her family but not be so personally involved." He paused. "I know you better than that though."

Aaron released a heavy sigh and gazed at the flames licking at the fresh log he'd placed in the fire.

"I love her, Tim." He shrugged as the confession just slipped out. "I know it's a mess of a situation, and I've brought it on myself, but I can't help it. I don't know what it means for the future, I just know that, right now, I have to make sure she and that baby are all right. If that means losing friends and respect . . ." He shook his head, a weight pressing down on his heart. "I don't know what else to do."

"I know." Timothy smiled faintly, heartening Aaron. "And, no matter what happens, I'll always be behind you."

EVEN AFTER THREE days, Gwen still talked about the meeting. Of all of them, Lacy knew she would be the one to make friends the easiest. People always found her smile and friendly nature infectious, thankfully. Lacy hoped it would stay this way for both Gwen and Hannah—that people wouldn't consider them tainted by their sister's sins.

However, it wasn't only the new friends that had them so enthused but Timothy's message. The two of them had even begun a dedicated study of the King's Scrolls in the mornings. Their mother had happily joined them. Lacy, however, always found something to do during that awkward hour. It wasn't that she didn't wish to be part of it, but she had strayed so far—sunk so deeply. She would never be worthy of joining them. It was too late for that.

While they sat around the kitchen table for this morning's study, Lacy gathered her sewing kit and a dress to modify and settled alone in the living room. Her sister's voices hummed from the other room as they took turns reading and discussing. Lacy fought to silence the pang of longing that welled inside her and focused on her work.

Half an hour later, someone knocked at the door. Lacy set her sewing aside and rose to answer it. Aaron came by every day to check on them. Her spirit lifted a little in anticipation. Seeing him would help alleviate some of the heaviness inside of her.

She pulled the door open with a smile, but it dropped upon seeing the stranger on their doorstep. Her heart crashed into her ribs, fear washing through her. Had Mr. Darwin sent someone new? She fought to still the panic.

"Can I help you?"

"I am Matthias Artel." He peered at her and leaned back slightly as if trying to keep as much space between them as possible. "I am a friend of Mr. Silvar."

Now that the fear of Mr. Darwin had passed, Lacy did recognize him. She had seen Aaron talking to him at the meeting.

"Would you like to come in?" She shifted and gestured into the house.

However, he looked decidedly uncomfortable with this invitation. "No, thank you. But I would like to speak to you."

Lacy frowned at his cool tone, and her stomach twisted. She swallowed down her apprehension. "Let me get my coat."

She turned into the entryway and took it from the peg. As she slipped it on and stepped outside with Mr. Artel, she had to wonder what kind of man would make a pregnant woman stand outside in the cold when they could have just as easily gone inside.

He backed away as she closed the door, keeping several feet between them as he peered down at her. Now she recognized the disapproval in his expression and braced herself.

The man drew himself up. "Miss…"

"Evern."

"Miss Evern," he began again, his tone very businesslike, "I and others of my congregation are concerned about your…dealings with Mr. Silvar."

Lacy's spine prickled and stiffened. "I have not had *dealings* with Mr. Silvar, as you put it. Aaron has been an incredible help to my family and to me. If not for him, my child would be dead, and I would still be…" Heat rose up her neck and into her cheeks. She dropped her gaze and cleared her throat before forcing herself to look up at the man again. "He has been very kind to me, my sisters, and my mother."

"At great cost to his reputation," the man said grimly.

Lacy suppressed a wince, but irritation rose with it. "Do you not trust Aaron's integrity?"

The man lifted his chin as if he were the moral authority on the subject. "Any man can be tempted. Skirting around the very edges of danger is never a wise decision, especially when the object of temptation constantly dangles itself in front of you."

Lacy's cheeks burned again, and she clenched her teeth. She had never *dangled* herself in front of Aaron. She had fought to do the exact opposite, in fact, desperate for him to see her as more than an object men used and discarded without thought. And he had. Not only did he see past all of it, but he had saved her from that life. He'd restored her broken belief that men of honor did exist. How dare this man question that honor.

"What about you, sir? Do you think your congregation should be concerned about you showing up at the door of a known prostitute?"

The man sputtered. "I am only here to speak to you about Mr. Silvar's welfare."

"And Aaron is only here because of my family's welfare. I can assure you, his intentions are no less honorable than yours, sir." Not that she considered this man to be particularly honorable at the moment.

"Be that as it may, you are hurting his reputation amongst those who have looked up to him. If you care at all, then tell him to stay away."

Lacy's heart missed a beat. Tell Aaron to stay away?

"If we are being blunt, Miss Evern," the man went on, "he can aid your family without endangering his reputation in your presence."

Lacy's eyes smarted. It was true, but the thought of not seeing him again hurt almost enough to take her breath away. "Aaron makes his own decisions."

"Yet, I have no doubt you could sway him."

Lacy breathed hard. She might not be tempting Aaron in some ways, at least not intentionally, but was she in others? Was she swaying him to make poor decisions? She swallowed the lump in her throat.

"I'll tell him what you've said. After that, the choice is his."

"I hope you'll encourage him to make the right choice." He gave her only a curt nod in farewell and turned away without another word.

"If I were you, I would take it easy for another couple of weeks at least."

Aaron remained silent at the physician's suggestion. Now that Rodin had cleared him of any ill effects of a concussion, it was time to get back to work. First thing in the morning, he would be back down at the docks. His ribs might torture him every step of the way, but it was just the price he'd have to pay.

He glanced at Timothy, who gave him a look that said he knew exactly what Aaron was intending. However, Timothy only offered the physician a smile.

"Thanks for stopping in to check on him."

Rodin nodded and packed up his medical bag. After he had left, Aaron pushed up from his chair at the kitchen table. He helped Timothy clean what was left from their lunch, and then walked into the entry and reached for his coat.

"I'm going to see Lacy," he told his brother. He had some money to give them. Ben had come by earlier with as much as he could offer from a recent sale in merchandise. He could only pray that it and what more he could earn at the docks in the next few days would be enough to change Darwin's mind about wanting the debt paid off now. It would certainly be more than Lacy's usual payments. If they could just hang on until the weather turned warm. Then Aaron could take Lacy and her family to Landale and contend with the debt without fear of one of them being thrown in a workhouse.

Outside, an icy breeze reminded Aaron that warm weather was still a ways off. Clouds gathered heavily overhead. No doubt it would snow. Winter wasn't done with them just yet. However, the thought of the warm hearth in the Everns' kitchen spurred him on. The house might be small and bare, but the women still succeeded in making it a warm home.

When he arrived, Lacy answered the door as she usually did. Though she smiled, it failed to reach her eyes.

"Something wrong?"

He followed her inside, where she peeked up at him but didn't hold his gaze. "I had a visitor this morning."

Aaron stiffened. "One of Darwin's men?"

She shook her head. "Someone from your congregation."

He lifted his brows. Someone from the congregation had come here to see Lacy? His stomach constricted, and he clenched his fists. If whoever it was had come seeking her company, he was going to hit them so hard—

"It's not like that," Lacy said.

He let out his breath slowly and flexed his fingers, only marginally relieved. Before he could question her, Gwen stepped into the hall to greet him. He hid his agitation as he hung up his coat and followed both of them into the kitchen. Once he had greeted the rest of the family, he turned his focus to Lacy. He wanted to get to the bottom of the mystery guest. Everything about her face told him it wasn't a kindhearted visit of goodwill toward Lacy and her family.

Looking at her mother, Lacy said, "I need to talk to Aaron."

Helen nodded, and Lacy led Aaron into the living room. She stopped near the fireplace, rubbing her hands together as she stared at the flames. Aaron crossed his arms.

"Who was it?"

She turned to him. "Mr. Artel."

Matthias? Aaron couldn't imagine him coming near this place. "He came here?"

"Well, he came to the door. He was very adamant about staying outside."

Of course. "What did he want?"

Lacy looked down at her hands that she now rested on her stomach. Her eyes were pained as she lifted them to his face once more.

"He made it very clear that I am putting your reputation in great jeopardy. He believes that you should stay away from me…and that I should encourage you to."

Aaron let his arms drop and squeezed his fists again. If Matthias was so concerned, then he should have come to Aaron—not dragged Lacy into this. He didn't doubt Matthias had his best interest in mind, but the way he'd gone about it didn't make Aaron feel very charitable toward him.

"Never mind what he said. I have no problem coming here to see you."

"What if…" He heard her breath catch as she swallowed. "What if I want you to stay away?" She would only hold his gaze for a moment.

Aaron tilted his head. "Then I'd say you were lying."

Her gaze snapped up, and he gave her a small smile, hoping to draw hers out. However, the sadness remained in her eyes.

"But it is true that I don't want to ruin your reputation. You're a good man, Aaron—the best man I've ever known. I can't bear the thought of changing that."

"You're not." He reached up and put his hands on her shoulders. She stared at him intently. "I don't care about people's opinions. I never have. And I have many other friends who know me well and who I respect above all others. I'm not worried about my reputation with them. You don't have to be either."

She remained silent for a moment before she murmured, "I just don't want to cause you to make choices you will regret."

"Any choices I make are on me, not you." He squeezed her shoulders and smiled again. This time her smile peeked through. "So don't worry, I can handle it."

Lacy nodded, her expression relaxing. Her lovely eyes cleared of concern, and she motioned to a chair. "Why don't you sit down? I'll get you some coffee."

Aaron accepted the invitation. He had nowhere else to be until tomorrow when it was back to work.

A couple of minutes later, Lacy brought a hot cup of coffee from the kitchen, and her mother and sisters followed. As snow started to fall outside, they sat around the fire and talked, laughing and sharing stories. Aaron found himself watching Lacy most of the time. He didn't think he'd ever seen her smile so much. He would do whatever he could to make sure she continued to smile often.

The afternoon passed comfortably. Before he knew it, evening had set in. Helen rose from her chair and said, "I should get supper going. Will you join us, Aaron?"

"I wouldn't want to overstay my welcome." He'd be more than happy to remain, but he had been here for hours already.

Helen shook her head. "Nonsense. Please stay."

Aaron smiled. "I'd love to."

With a smile of her own, Helen went off to the kitchen, and Hannah and Gwen soon followed to help her. Aaron slid from his chair and knelt at the fireplace to put a couple more pieces of wood on the glowing embers. Sitting back, he stared up at Lacy, who was curled up on her chair and leaning against a pillow. She looked a little sleepy but content, her cheeks rosy with the fire's warmth. Her hand rested over her stomach, rubbing it gently.

She met his eyes and held them for a quiet moment. Finally, Aaron asked, "What do you think it will be? A boy or a girl?"

Her lips lifted happily. "A boy." Then she shrugged. "At least, I'm hoping it's a boy. It's about time after all of us girls."

Aaron smiled. He could picture her with a little boy. "He'd be very unfairly outnumbered."

Lacy giggled. "True, but he'd also be completely spoiled." She looked down at her stomach, her brows pulling together. "He would need someone to teach him how to be a good man."

Something reacted inside of Aaron. He could do that.

Before he could say a word, Lacy sucked in a quick breath, her hand stilling over her stomach. She looked at him again and beckoned him closer. "Come here."

He pushed to his knees and moved closer to her chair.

"Give me your hand."

He did so, and she placed it against her stomach. Beneath the layers of her dress, something thumped against his palm. He lifted his brows and looked up into her face. A wide smile bloomed.

"He's kicking."

Aaron's grin broke out as he felt it again—the life inside her. The little child who would soon come into the world. The throbbing sensation in his chest grew with the desire to make sure he or she would never want for anything and would be sheltered from the hardships that surrounded them. The same desire he had for Lacy. He looked into her eyes. He had never met anyone like her. She was so strong, so…beautiful. His gaze dropped to her lips, and he leaned closer. She tipped her head down, her forehead almost resting against his. His heart pounded with her nearness.

Just before their lips touched, a little squeak came from the doorway. Aaron pulled back, and they both found Gwen standing in the doorway. Her mouth hung open for a moment before she stammered, "I, uh, just wanted to know…never mind."

She spun around and rushed out. Aaron turned back to Lacy. She had her head bent, her cheeks bright pink, but a little smile on her lips.

"I'd better see what she wants."

Smiling to himself as well, Aaron pushed to his feet and helped her up. As he followed her to the kitchen, his heart still thumped inside his chest. He'd never been so close to a woman before and certainly not one he had ever felt so strongly for.

AARON SUCKED IN a breath, gritted his teeth, and dragged a sack of grain off a wagon. Slinging it over his shoulder, he swallowed down a groan. The bandages he'd wrapped around his chest to support his ribs didn't help much, but he'd dealt with the pain for a week now, and he'd keep doing it, one day at a time, until his ribs healed. Whatever it took to keep on working.

He turned for the warehouse, where other workers arranged the grain sacks. In the bustle of activity, he spotted a familiar face weaving toward him through the crowded wharf. He froze. It was Tavor. Ice built in the pit of his stomach.

When the man reached him, the regret in his eyes said everything. "Banson and his men returned. There were too many of them to stop. They've taken Mrs. Evern."

The grain sack slid from Aaron's shoulder and hit the ground with a heavy thud. He'd failed. Despite everything he had done to try to protect Lacy and her family, they had taken Helen anyway.

"Is there a problem, Silvar?"

Aaron turned to the man overseeing the unloading of the wagon. "An emergency. I have to go."

He didn't wait; he just followed Tavor through the crowd. He had to get to Lacy. Hc had to make sure she was all right. Then he had to see Darwin and somehow get Helen safely back to her daughters before the worst happened. *Please protect her!* The weather was still far too cold for her to be out. Without warmth or the remedy she always used to soothe her lungs, she could die at any time.

Aaron broke into a jog as soon as they were out of the crowd and did not stop until he reached the Evern house. A bit of blood spattered the snow near the door. Did it belong to one of Banson's or Avery's men? Or could it be Helen's or Lacy's?

He pulled the door open and rushed inside. The mournful sounds of weeping guided him into the living room. Timothy, Ben, and Mira were already there. Aaron glanced to his left where Avery stood in the corner, an apologetic look on his face. But Aaron's attention locked on Lacy. Tears poured down her cheeks as she looked up at him from where she huddled on the couch with her sisters and Mira. The broken hopelessness in her watery eyes pierced Aaron's chest.

He stepped toward her. She rose up to meet him, and he took her in his arms. She wept into his shoulder, clinging to him.

"I'm sorry," he murmured in her ear. "I'm so sorry." He didn't know what else to say. He'd done what he'd believed to be right, but those actions had still led to this. He had promised to take care of things. The only way to fix it now would be to get their mother back.

He let Lacy cry for a couple of minutes. Once her heart-breaking sobs quieted, he pulled away gently and looked down into her face.

"I'll go talk to Darwin."

A desperate hope flared in her eyes that it would kill him to disappoint. One way or another, he had to save Helen.

However, Lacy's face crumpled again. "He has never listened to us before."

Aaron rubbed her arms. "He's never talked to me." He forced a confident smile.

She didn't smile in return, but she did appear heartened.

Lord, please don't let me disappoint her.

He glanced at Timothy and the others. "I'll go see him now."

Lacy returned to her seat with her sisters, and Ben and Timothy stepped toward him.

"I'll go with you," Ben said.

Aaron nodded and then looked at Timothy. "Why don't you stay with them?"

Timothy had always been a comforting and encouraging presence in hard times.

With a nod, he turned back to the women. Aaron traded one more look with Lacy, and then left the room with Ben. Avery followed.

Outside, he said, "I'm sorry about what happened. My men tried to stop it, but Banson came prepared."

"I'm sure they did everything they could," Aaron responded. He'd been under no illusions that Avery's men could keep Banson away forever. He'd only hoped it would buy them a bit more time.

They parted with Avery, and Aaron strode with Ben through the streets toward Darwin's residence.

Lacy had not dealt with such devastating emotions since her father had died. Their mother was the force that had held them all together. With her gone, Lacy didn't know what they would do, especially with the baby coming. She needed her mother like never before. She couldn't raise a child without her mother's knowledge to guide her.

The spark of hope that had grown inside of her seemed to have left with Aaron. How could he possibly convince Mr. Darwin to change his mind? Men like that didn't care what happened to anyone as long as they got what they wanted. Why would he even listen to Aaron?

Lacy scrunched her eyes closed and clutched her stomach as nausea threatened to upturn it. Tears burned against her eyelids. What if her mother died? She or one of her sisters would have to take her place. She couldn't bear to see one of her sisters dragged off like that, but if she volunteered, what would happen to the baby? And who would take care of Hannah and Gwen?

Aaron would.

But the baby. Surely, she would lose it in the workhouse's awful living conditions and being worked like a slave.

Her tears leaked from her eyes and burned her cheeks. Unless Aaron changed Mr. Darwin's mind, she was going to lose someone. Her mother, one of her sisters, or her baby. Maybe more than one. The pain of it pressed down heavily on her chest.

"We should pray."

Lacy opened her eyes. She had forgotten that Timothy was still there.

"Yes," Mira agreed. "Prayer is the strongest weapon we have right now."

Hannah and Gwen eagerly responded. Lacy felt her own soul desperate to cry out to Elôm to save her mother. Only such divine intervention could right this now. However, how could such a stained soul even dare to approach God? Lacy had sold her body away and sullied her soul in the process, even if it was purely out of desperation to provide for her family. Surely her broken prayers would mean nothing.

As her sisters bowed their heads to pray with Timothy and Mira for their mother, an ache built inside Lacy's heart. It grew so fierce she couldn't take it any longer.

Pushing to her feet, she fled the room. In the kitchen, she sank down into a chair, her tears flowing faster than she could wipe them away. Could this be her fault? Her punishment for what she had done? How could she ever make it right?

The floor creaked, and she looked up. Timothy stood in the doorway. The deep compassion in his eyes only fed her tears.

"You can join us," he said gently.

She shook her head. "No, I can't."

"Why not?"

"Because," Lacy choked out with a sob, "I'm unworthy."

Timothy stepped to the table and set a chair in front of her to sit down. Lacy had never seen a kindlier face.

"We don't come to Elôm because we are worthy; we come to Him because we *need* Him."

Lacy closed her eyes again. Her mother and sisters had all come to trust in Elôm, and she would teach her child to trust in Him, but after everything, surely it was too late for her.

"I'm soiled," she cried. "I've given myself away countless times. How could Elôm ever want me?"

Timothy reached for her hand—a comforting, caring gesture so different from what she had come to expect from men. "Let me tell you about a friend of mine. When he was fifteen, he murdered a man. After that, he was turned into a gladiator and killed many more men in the arenas. When I first met him, his past and the shame of it tortured him. He didn't even know if he had a soul, and many times he didn't even want to live anymore. He thought the blood on his hands was too great for him to ever be worthy of love or forgiveness. Nearly two years ago, he stood on the execution platform here in Valcré in front of a massive crowd who screamed for the emperor to kill him.

"My friend was considered the lowest and vilest of society. You see, not only was he a murderer, but he is also half ryrik. To the crowd, he didn't deserve to live. However, a man willingly traded places with him. This man was completely innocent, yet He *chose* to die in my friend's place."

Memories poured into Lacy's mind. She'd heard this story—at least part of it. Men had spoken of it for days in the tavern. No one could understand why anyone would die for a ryrik.

"Do you know who this man was?" Timothy asked.

Lacy shook her head slowly. From what she'd heard, He was just a fool.

"His name is Elon. He is the Son of Elôm. He took Jace's place because, regardless of Jace's past, regardless of the murder, regardless of the despair Jace lived in for so long, Elôm loves him. Loves him so much that Elon willingly sacrificed Himself so that Jace could live and be free of not only the mistakes of his past but all those of his future. Elon died on that platform in Jace's place. But it was even more than that. He died not only for Jace but for me, and for Aaron, and for all who seek Him. He died to remove the sins of your past and your future, no matter how great. All you have to do is accept it. It is a free gift of grace. A gift He wants to give you. There is nothing in your life that could cause Him to withhold it."

Lacy's whole being longed for forgiveness—for love, for hope. "But how could He possibly love someone so broken?"

Timothy squeezed her hand and gave her a small smile. "My brother loves you. And if he can love you, then why not an infinite God and Creator who wants only the best for His creation? Aaron has already looked beyond your past. Now let Elon wash it away completely."

Aaron followed a servant into Darwin's grand town-house and asked Elôm for wisdom. He had no real plan going into this. His only recourse was to appeal to Darwin's sympathies. Surely, he couldn't be so completely heartless as to condemn a sick woman to death in a workhouse even after listening to a plea for her release. But then, Aaron had known men who would do just that. His gut feeling was that this meeting would not go nearly as well as he hoped. Elôm would have to intervene.

Aaron glanced around as a footman led him and Ben through the house. The copious amount of art pointed to Darwin's wealth.

Off the main hall, the footman guided them through a large door and into a spacious office, where he announced their presence. Darwin sat behind an elaborate desk, books and parchments spread out around him. Several stacks of gold coins sat just to his left. He eyed them with stern eyes and set the quill pen in his hand aside.

"What can I do for you?"

His cool tone suggested that he actually meant, "What can I do to get you to leave quickly?"

Aaron stepped forward. "I'm here about Helen Evern."

Annoyance flashed across the man's lined face. "What about her?"

"You must have her released."

The man snorted, and then rose, sizing Aaron up. He was about a head taller than Aaron, and despite being a merchant, stood with a confidence that said he could handle himself.

"You're the one causing all the trouble with that family, Mister...."

Aaron hesitated for a heartbeat before providing a name. "Carliss." He and Timothy had used their mother's maiden name for years while living in the Graylin Valley. He didn't want the name Silvar filtering back to the queen.

"Mr. Carliss, are you aware of the money they owe me?"

Aaron nodded. "Yes."

"Then why did you take that girl away from her job?"

"She is with child. She couldn't have kept working there."

"Oh, she very well could have if you had not stepped in and swayed her decisions. Our arrangement was just fine before that."

Aaron gritted his teeth. "You will still get your money. Just let Mrs. Evern go."

"And where will this money come from?"

"From me."

The man just smirked at him. "What guarantees do I have of that?"

"You have my word."

Now the man actually laughed. "You think your word means anything to me?"

Before Aaron could retort, Ben was at his side.

"I'll vouch for him." Apparently Ben had some acquaintance with Mr. Darwin, which wasn't surprising considering he was a merchant. "He will see that the debt is paid."

Darwin leveled him with a sharp look. "Word has it that your own finances are not what they used to be."

Of course, the only reason for this was that he and Mira gave so much to the congregation, but they couldn't tell Darwin that.

When Ben did not reply immediately, Darwin returned his attention to Aaron. "I think we're done here."

But Aaron wasn't. He took another step closer to the

desk. "Were you aware of Mrs. Evern's lung condition when you sent Banson after her? If she stays in that workhouse, she'll be dead in a day or two."

"Then one or all of her daughters can take her place."

Anger boiled up inside Aaron, but Darwin continued before he could put up further protest.

"This is not a charity house, Mr. Carliss. Isaac Evern knew the risks when he borrowed from me. I've given those women over two years to pay that debt. I'm tired of waiting around and listening to excuses."

Aaron balled his fists. It was probably a good thing the desk sat between them. "You don't care who does it or how it's done, do you? All you care about is the money."

"That's right, Mr. Carliss," the man responded, leaning over the desk to look Aaron in the eyes. "I'm a business-man, and this is business."

Aaron resisted the urge to take action against him and contemplated the thoughts rushing through his mind. He glanced at Ben. This might not go over well, but what other choice did he have? He sent out a desperate prayer to Elôm and then straightened and faced Darwin again.

"If that's the case, then I'll work off their debt for them."

Darwin's eyes narrowed. "What?"

"Let Mrs. Evern go free, and I'll take her place in the workhouse. As you said, you don't care who works it off. With me, you'll see that money a lot faster. You're looking at what, four or five years before you see it all? Well, I bet I can get it back to you in two. I was a miner in Dunlow. I can work hard."

Aaron saw Ben hang his head out of the corner of his eye, but he kept his gaze locked with Darwin.

The man's smirk slowly returned to his face. "Very well, Mr. Carliss. If you want to trade your freedom for a harlot and her family, be my guest."

Aaron locked his teeth down on the retort that wanted to burst out. He gave a stiff nod. "You'll release Mrs. Evern then?"

"Yes."

"And your men will not harass her or her daughters again." This was a statement, not a question.

Now the man nodded. "Once you take her place, this will be between you and me. I want no more dealings with them."

With this agreement, both relief and heaviness descended on Aaron. Forcing aside the sick ache spreading inside him, he asked, "When will Mrs. Evern be released?"

"Banson will meet you at the workhouse in an hour. I suggest you use that time to make any arrangements you need to tend to."

With another nod, Aaron turned to follow the footman out.

One hour.

He had one hour of freedom left, and he intended to use it in the best way he could.

BOTH AARON AND Ben remained silent on the walk back to the Evern house. Ben said nothing about Aaron's decision—whether he thought it was a good move or a bad one. But Aaron was confident in the choice he had made. He felt no uncertainty, no regret. He still held firmly to the belief that he'd done right by helping Lacy leave the tavern, but if consequences must still be paid, then he would pay them.

However, he did have one difficult obstacle to face that sickened his stomach: telling Timothy and Lacy. Timothy would understand—Aaron was sure he would—but it would still be hard for them.

Finally, Aaron broke the silence. "Can Lacy and her family stay with you and Mira? I want to know they are well taken care of and that Lacy has everything she needs for the baby."

Without Aaron working, they would have no income.

"Of course," Ben replied without the slightest hesitation. "They'll be as safe as we can possibly make them."

Aaron looked the older man in the eyes. "Thank you." At least while he was locked away in the workhouse, he would have this comfort.

When they neared the Evern's, Ben paused and turned to Aaron. "I'll get a carriage to take the girls to our house and then to get Mrs. Evern. It will be better for her not to have to walk in this cold."

Aaron thanked him again. They parted, and he walked the rest of the way by himself. At the door, he drew in a deep breath before entering. He stepped into the living room, and all eyes locked on him expectantly. He let a small smile grow.

"Darwin is going to release her."

Lacy let out a cry, and she and her sisters burst into fresh tears, though this time of joy and relief. The sight affirmed to Aaron that he was doing the right thing.

Thankfully, none of them asked for details. He wanted to get them settled at Ben and Mira's before he broke the news to them. It didn't leave much time.

He focused on Lacy. "I'm going to the workhouse in an hour to get her. Right now, I need you to pack up your belongings. You are all going to stay with Ben and Mira for now."

Aaron glanced at Mira, but she showed no reaction to the news. The woman would be more than happy to take them in.

A frown marred Lacy's face. "Why?"

"It's the safest place for you, especially with the baby coming," Aaron told her. "You'll have everything you need. Ben will be here with a carriage shortly. Whatever you can't bring with you now, you can come back for later."

Though confusion remained on her face, Lacy nodded and motioned for her sisters to follow. They left the room, and Aaron waited until he heard them go upstairs before he faced Timothy. Already a knowing look had settled in his eyes.

With another steadying breath, Aaron broke the news. "Listen, Tim, I had to do something you probably won't like, but I had no choice. I offered to work off the debt in Helen's place."

Timothy absorbed this for a silent moment. "That will take time."

Aaron winced. "Two years, at least."

Though his expression was grim, Timothy nodded without protesting.

Still, it left Aaron cold inside. "I'm sorry I won't be around to watch over you like I promised Father. I just don't see any other way."

A hint of a sad smile came to his brother's face. "Don't worry. I can take care of myself. And when I can't, Elôm can. Do what you have to do."

Aaron reached out for his brother's shoulder and gave it a tight squeeze. "Thank you."

He looked over at Mira, whose eyes filled with tears. His throat tightened, but he cleared it. He couldn't let the emotion set in now.

"Aaron."

He returned his attention to his brother.

"I had a long talk with Lacy while you were gone."

Aaron's pulse quickened with an instinctive hope, but he didn't dare let it fully form. However, the beginnings of the smile on Timothy's face made him hold his breath.

"She has turned to Elôm."

That clog in Aaron's throat returned with a vengeance, making his nose sting and his eyes water. It wasn't nearly so easy to force away this time. Timothy's smile grew, and Aaron's broke out.

"Thanks," he murmured, though his voice was strangled. This made things so much easier. It was everything he'd hoped for and reinforced the decision he had already made subconsciously.

A few minutes later, Lacy and her sisters returned, lugging canvas bags full of their belongings. Aaron quickly reached for Lacy's. She looked up at him. Though redness still rimmed her eyes from crying, relief softened all her features. Aaron could have just stared at her for days. However, they had less than an hour.

Her forehead wrinkled just slightly at his intense gaze, and he made himself smile. As soon as they reached Ben and Mira's they would talk.

Ben arrived shortly. Aaron and Timothy helped the girls make their final preparations and then escorted them to the carriage. Timothy crawled up to sit with the driver to make room inside for the rest of them. Along the way, Mira went to great lengths to assure the girls that she and Ben were delighted to have them stay. Aaron watched Lacy from his seat next to Ben. She looked so happy with the assurance that they would provide everything needed for her pregnancy. He let out a long breath. After the last couple of weeks, he would finally be sure of Lacy's wellbeing. That was worth a hundred years of imprisonment.

When they reached the house, Aaron climbed out first and turned to help Lacy, holding her gently around the waist to make sure she didn't lose her footing. His hands didn't want to let go once she was on the ground, but the others were waiting to get out.

Aaron and Ben carried the bags inside, and Mira led them all into the living room where it was warm. Here, silence fell, as if even the walls of the room knew something was going on. Aaron wanted to give the girls a little time to settle in, but they didn't have such time. Once he left, he would not come back. They needed to know of the arrangement.

Lacy turned to him. Though she had not asked any questions, she seemed to sense the things that weren't said. "Are you going to get my mother?"

Aaron nodded. "Yes, in just a few minutes." He paused, gathering all the strength he had. "Ben will bring her back here to you, but...I will have to stay."

Her skin turned pale, and she visibly swallowed. "What do you mean?"

"I made a deal with Darwin. I'm taking your mother's place to work off the debt."

Moisture gushed into her eyes and leaked from the corners. She shook her head and cried softly, "No."

Her shoulders shook as sobs gripped her. Her sisters burst into tears as well.

Their sorrow was a painful fuel to the ache engulfing his chest. He reached up and cupped Lacy's face in his hands so that she would look at him. He knew it was painful, but they had to understand.

"It's all right," he said, looking into her eyes. "Everything will be all right. It's only for a couple of years. You'll all be safe. The debt will be paid off and you won't have to worry about it again."

"But it shouldn't have to be you," Lacy cried mournfully.

Aaron smiled at her. "I'm happy to do it. Just trust me that it will be all right."

She closed her eyes, the tears still leaking through, but then she nodded against his hands.

Wiping her cheeks with his thumbs, he let his hands fall to her shoulders. He glanced around the room. Everyone seemed resigned to what he had to do. Now he had to get his personal business settled before he ran out of time. His heart gave another heavy thump as he looked down at Lacy again.

"I need to talk to you alone."

She drew a shaky breath but nodded.

Aaron let his hand slide down her arm and took her hand in his. Turning, he guided her toward the door. He led her to a small parlor just down the hall and closed the door. When he turned to face her, she looked unsure, but he had never been so certain in his life.

"I only have a few minutes before I have to go, but I need to ask you something. Once I'm free and this is all over…will you marry me?"

Her eyes grew wide with genuine surprise, but the uncertainty only grew. "Aaron…"

He stopped her. "Before you answer, I want you to know that I love you. I have for a long time and have wanted you as my wife for almost as long. But I don't want you to say yes just because of what I'm doing for your mother. I'll happily do this regardless of your answer. I only want you to say yes if you feel the same way I do."

Lacy looked away from him, a clear struggle on her face. He waited quietly, though he couldn't read her expression—whether she loved him too or cared about him only as a friend. It would hurt significantly if it was the latter, but that wouldn't change how much he cared about her.

At last, she spoke, her gaze dropping to the floor. "You deserve better."

Aaron drew a breath to speak, but she continued.

"When I took that job at the tavern, I did it with full knowledge and certainty that no good man would ever want me. I've made peace with that."

"Maybe, but I haven't."

Lacy gave her head a sad shake. "You should have a woman who hasn't been with dozens of other men and isn't carrying a child with no idea who the father even is. You should have a wife carrying *your* child."

"He will be my child. I don't care who his father is." Aaron stepped closer to her. "And I'm sure we'll have others. If we marry, whatever children are part of our life I will consider my own, whether they have my blood or not. I promise you that."

Tears tracked down Lacy's face, and she still wouldn't look up at him. "I'm damaged, Aaron. You deserve more than a scarred bride. I've already done enough damage to your reputation."

Hang his reputation. Those who truly knew him and were his friends were the only ones who mattered. People would believe what they wanted. He wasn't afraid to love her, and he would show her that.

He cupped her damp cheek in his hand and tipped her face up. Their eyes locked for a brief moment before he bent to kiss her. He had never kissed a woman before. She was soft, and warm, and encompassed every dream he didn't even realize he'd had. And he wasn't afraid of the past or the future.

He broke the kiss with effort and gazed down at her. "Scars don't bother me. We all have them. We're all broken in some way. Love is finding the ways our broken pieces fit together. If Elôm can love us as messed up as we are, we can love each other."

Lacy stared up at him and everything changed in her expression, a beautiful serenity replaced the uncertainty. "Yes," she whispered. "I will marry you."

Joy burst through Aaron, breaking out in a grin. She smiled back at him—the same smile he had fallen so hopelessly in love with the moment he had first set eyes on her. He pulled her close and kissed her again. He didn't want to stop. He never wanted to stop. But time stood against them. He pulled away, breathing hard. He would have married her today if he had not had to leave.

"As soon as I get back, then."

"As soon as you get back," she repeated in a quiet murmur.

He stared at her for another moment, brushing back her hair and letting his fingers trace her face as he soaked in every detail of it. He then let his hand fall to her swollen belly where he had felt the baby kick. Lacy rested her hand over his, and that's when he let it sink in. He was going to be a father. This little boy or girl would be his child. A child he wouldn't even meet until it was a toddler.

That relentless vise squeezed his throat and chest again. He wouldn't see the first smile, first steps, first words.

Wouldn't be able to hold his newborn baby. Yet all of that was why he had to do this—so that the baby would have a life and be safe. So that his child *would* smile and laugh and walk.

He took a deep breath and let this strengthen him. "I have to go."

She squeezed his hand as if to keep him there, but then she let it slide away, and they left the room. Rejoining the others, Aaron said nothing about their conversation. Lacy could give her sisters the news once he was gone. Now didn't seem to be the time to make an announcement of their betrothal. First they had to face the years they would spend apart.

In a silent, solemn group, they gathered outside by the waiting carriage. Aaron turned to face everyone. He started with Mira, giving the older woman a hug and thanking her for being so willing to watch over Lacy and her sisters while he was gone. Though she was in tears by the end, she had strong words of encouragement for him. He then moved on to Hannah and Gwen. Both of them cried as they traded goodbyes, and it grew harder for him to maintain his own composure. In the last weeks, they had become everything he'd ever imagined sisters to be.

Finally, he reached Lacy again. Her cheeks were wet, but hope for their future seemed to have strengthened her to face this parting. He slipped his arms around her and held her close. She hugged him tightly, her hands gripping the back of his coat. And between them, their child. Aaron closed his eyes and prayed for the safety of his future family.

"Thank you for doing this for us," Lacy's voice

murmured in his ear. She paused just briefly, and then said, "I love you."

Aaron smiled, despite the way his eyes stung. He pulled away enough to look down into her face. "You will wait for me?"

"I'll wait forever for you."

Her sure declaration was all that he needed. He pressed his forehead against hers, savoring these last fleeting moments of nearness to her before he stepped back.

"Be careful...please." Her voice broke.

Aaron nodded firmly. "I will."

However, they both knew not everyone survived the workhouse. Not even some of the strong ones. But he would survive this. He had too much waiting for him here.

He backed toward the carriage. "Goodbye." He swallowed hard. "I love you."

Lacy's lips trembled, and her eyes pooled. "Goodbye," she barely whispered.

With great difficulty, Aaron turned away, but the pain only intensified as he came face to face with Timothy. He wasn't sure he had another goodbye in him, especially when seeing the emotion in his brother's eyes.

"Ben and I will go with you to get Helen," Timothy said.

Aaron let out a sigh. This would give him a little time to regather his resolve.

They climbed into the carriage. As it pulled away, Aaron looked out the window at Lacy. She was crying now, and he wanted more than anything in the world to stay with her. A few seconds later, the carriage left the yard, and she disappeared from sight. Aaron's heart failed for a moment before painfully beating on. He sank back against the carriage and pressed his fingers to his eyes to keep the moisture burning there from leaking out. He had to do this, but it tore him up like nothing he'd ever had to do before.

A couple of minutes later, he wrestled his emotions back under control and looked up at Timothy. His brother appeared to be praying but quickly met Aaron's eyes.

"Lacy agreed to marry me once this is all over," Aaron told him.

A smile flickered on Timothy's face. "I'm glad. Anyone could see how much you love her, and it's obvious she loves you too."

"You know that will make you an uncle." It was better to focus on the future he had to look forward to than what he had to get through to reach it.

Timothy smiled again. "I'll like that."

"And maybe, by that time, I'll be close to being an uncle as well?"

Timothy chuckled quietly and glanced down at his hands. "Maybe."

Aaron smiled now. He hoped Timothy and Leetra would be married by then. It would be good for Timothy to have her at his side, especially now. Aaron would hate to miss the wedding though.

He forced these thoughts aside. They would not help him now.

Before he was ready, they arrived at the workhouse, and the carriage pulled to a stop. His heart sank toward his stomach, but concern for Helen quickly outweighed it. Every minute spent here could mean death. This propelled him to move, and he climbed out of the carriage first. He glanced up at the massive, dreary stone building in front of him before dropping his attention to the door. Banson stood there, a bit of a smirk on his face.

"You actually went through with it," he said.

Aaron gave a curt nod. "I'm here, now where's Mrs. Evern?"

With a smug look, Banson turned slowly and rapped his knuckle on the door. A moment later, it groaned open. Two men stepped out, guiding Helen. Aaron let out a long breath. She was pale and exhausted but still very much alive. Thank Elôm.

The men released her, and she walked straight to Aaron. Tears filled her eyes.

"They told me what you're doing." She wrapped her icy fingers around his. "You shouldn't have to do this."

Aaron gave her a smile. "I'm happy to. You're going to have a grandbaby you need to be around for."

A smile reached her face as well, though it trembled and a couple of tears rolled down her cheeks.

Aaron squeezed her cold hands. "Let's get you inside the carriage where it's warmer."

He turned, and he and Ben helped her up and into the carriage.

Now it was time for the final goodbyes.

Aaron turned to Ben first. The man gave him warm encouragement that Aaron would make sure to carry with him into the workhouse. Then he faced Timothy.

He struggled for words. Finally, he just put his arms around his brother and hauled him into a crushing embrace.

After a moment, Timothy murmured, "You are the strongest and most resilient person I've ever known. I know you'll make it through this."

Aaron swallowed hard. Blast that burning in his eyes and throat. It prevented him from speaking, and he could only nod against his brother's shoulder. They broke apart then. Aaron tried to smile, but it barely reached his lips.

"Take care of yourself," he forced out hoarsely.

Timothy's eyes glimmered with moisture. "You too."

Dragging together every shredded scrap of resolve, Aaron turned and walked toward Banson and the door to the workhouse. He did not let himself look back. To do so would break him. He stepped through the doorway. When the door closed behind him, a chill washed through his body, but steely determination joined it. The choice was made now. He couldn't turn back—he could only forge ahead. For Lacy.

Lacy peered out the window, waiting for the carriage to arrive with her mother. Hot, wet tears streamed down her cheeks. She rubbed her hand over her stomach as the baby moved inside her, and she bit back a sob that squeezed her chest. She could still feel Aaron's hand resting where hers was now. If she closed her eyes, she could imagine the gentle yet ardent way he'd held and kissed her. She had never let herself even dream of a future that involved real love, a husband, and a father for her child. To have it so close yet out of reach pierced her right to the core.

What if he did not come back? What if he never made it out of that workhouse?

Her tears flowed more heavily, and the sob finally broke free. "Elôm," she cried with it. She'd had less than an hour to even contemplate her newfound faith, but everything inside her yearned to cry out to the merciful and loving God that Aaron and his brother had painted such a vivid picture of. "Please protect him and bring him back to me."

AARON BEAT THE sledgehammer down over and over again until it became a mind-numbing motion that would fill up yet another day. The larger rocks at his feet shattered into smaller ones used to pave paths somewhere in Arcacia. He moved on to the next. And the next. The sun beat down and sent sweat rolling along his face and back. Sometime in the blur of days, spring had arrived. Though some nights he still thought he might freeze, the days grew much warmer. Not that the gray, enclosed courtyard of the workhouse showed any sign of the new life that must be blooming outside.

Aaron winced, the pain in his heart competing with the other aches and pains he'd collected. Had Lacy had their baby yet? Surely she was due any time now. He'd lost track of the days, but he guessed two months had passed since he'd given himself up for Helen.

Only two months.

He quickly buried these thoughts with any others like them. While he kept Lacy in the center of his mind to help keep himself going, he didn't let thoughts of what was happening outside this prison take hold for more than a moment. It was too painful to contemplate what he was missing and how far he had to go. The future was what he had to hang on to. Not the present.

He set the sledge down and turned to the never-ending heap of rocks to his left. As he selected another stone to break, he glanced around the colorless yard. Dozens of other men worked around him, all clothed in the same dirty gray work clothes. It was a wonder most of them hadn't died in the outbreak of the Miner's Fever over the winter, but he'd learned they had accepted years being added to their sentences here in exchange for the remedy. He prayed he would never have to make that choice. It could mean five years or more instead of two. He was determined not to let that happen. Two years would be hard enough. This place broke men. He could see it in the vacant eyes of those who had been here the longest. He couldn't let that happen to him—not if he wanted to be a good husband and father when he got out. He had to keep his hope and sanity intact, and he prayed for the strength to do that.

He picked up the sledgehammer again and prepared to swing it.

"Carliss!"

He looked over his shoulder. One of the wardens strode toward him. His insides constricted. The wardens didn't interrupt the prisoners' work unless there was trouble. He'd already received his first warning for stepping in and trying to help a fellow prisoner who could barely stand upright let alone do his work. However, he could think of nothing he'd done recently that would have riled them.

"Yes?"

The warden jerked his head toward the barracks the prisoners called home. "Come with me."

Aaron let the sledgehammer slip from his hand and bit his tongue upon the impulse to question the man. Whatever this was, he'd rather know ahead of time to prepare. However, silent obedience was the only way to avoid further trouble.

Bracing himself, he followed the man to the barracks. Inside, they passed through the sleeping quarters crammed full of bunks. Even with the sun shining, the air inside remained cold. The small fireplace smoldering at the other end didn't reach this far. With only one ratty blanket each, it was a miracle more men didn't freeze to death. Aaron already dreaded the thought of another winter.

They stepped through a door that was usually barred and then down a hall to the wardens' quarters. Aaron breathed a little easier. If they were going to whip him for something, they probably would have done it in the yard as an example to everyone. He had seen it happen often enough. Still, it didn't explain why he was here.

He scanned the room as the warden approached a desk. It was much warmer and better furnished in here, of course.

"Put these on."

Aaron's attention snapped back to the warden. A balled-up pile of clothing rested in his hands. Aaron lifted his brows. Those were his clothes—the ones he'd been wearing when he'd given himself up. Why would they give them back? He lifted his eyes to meet the warden's gaze.

"You're being set free."

Aaron's heart missed a beat. "What?" He couldn't have heard right, could he?

"Your debt's been paid." The man's face soured as if he was irritated about having to remain here.

Aaron stood speechless, his mind whirring. The debt was paid? How was that even possible? Had Timothy and Ben somehow collected the money? But, after only two months, that seemed unlikely, and Darwin certainly wouldn't have settled for anything less than the full amount.

"Well?" the warden barked.

Aaron snapped from the whirling questions and took his clothes. The only way to gain answers was to get out of here. He changed quickly. Though his clothing felt looser than he remembered, the familiarity was something he hadn't even realized how much he missed. He followed the warden again, through the halls and finally to the door he didn't think he'd see again for years. He paused as the man opened it, letting the sunlight stream in. The warden then just stared at him with impatient expectancy.

Would anyone be waiting on the other side of that door? What if this wasn't freedom at all? What if someone had discovered his identity and told the queen? There could be a whole company of royal guards standing right outside waiting to drag him away. Then he would never see Lacy or Timothy or the baby.

He drew in a heavy breath. There was only one way to find out.

He stepped through the door, squinting a little in the sun. No group of guards waited to surround him—just one person.

"Tim?"

His brother's face split into a wide smile. Aaron didn't know how this was possible, but he stepped forward and dragged his brother into his arms. He'd spent the last two months believing he wouldn't even see him again for years. Now, somehow, he was out and free. Emotion rushed in, and he had to squeeze his eyes shut to keep it contained.

Finally, they broke apart, and Aaron looked his brother in the eyes. "How did you do this?"

"You'll have to thank Avery for it. He got the money."

Aaron couldn't imagine how he'd collected it so quickly, but it all flew from his mind as something more important took its place.

"How is Lacy?"

"She is doing well."

"And the baby?"

Timothy's smile grew again. "Due any day now."

Aaron released a huge breath. He would be there for the birth. He hadn't missed it. His eyes slid closed for a moment, and he thanked Elôm. He had resigned himself to not seeing the child—his future child—until it was a couple of years old at least. Thanks to Elôm's grace, he wouldn't miss such a chunk of time.

"I need to see her." He turned in the direction of Ben and Mira's, but Timothy stopped him.

"Why don't we go home first and you can get cleaned up...and maybe eat something." His brow creased as he looked Aaron up and down.

Aaron wanted to protest, but he paused long enough to consider how rough his appearance must be and rubbed his knuckles over the beard that had grown along his jaw. There'd been little time to shave or see to any sort of personal hygiene in the workhouse. He supposed he probably should clean up for Lacy.

"That bad, huh?"

Timothy shrugged.

"All right."

Together, they set off through the city.

After several yards, Timothy asked, "So, how are you?"

Aaron let the question sink in for a moment before answering. "Tired, hungry, sore. And I'm sure I reek." He cast Timothy a quick grin, and his brother chuckled. But then they grew serious again. "I'm glad to be out of there."

He didn't have to say anything more. Timothy would understand. They both had firsthand knowledge of what it was like to live in squalor and have to work at a grueling pace. The workhouse wasn't all that much different from Dunlow, except that it lacked any sort of freedom.

Aaron quickly pushed these thoughts away. He was out now. The future he had been dreaming of was right in front of him. He would focus on that and the blessing of it. His pace quickened. Timothy had to lengthen his stride to keep up, but Aaron couldn't suppress his eagerness to get cleaned up and see Lacy. Would she be as happy to see him as he would be to see her? It had only been a couple of months, but what if she had second thoughts about getting married? He shook his head to himself. Why worry about that now?

Instead, he asked Timothy about any news from camp and about the members of their congregation. According to his brother, many of those who had questioned his involvement with Lacy, including Matthias, had begun to soften on the issue since he'd given himself up to work off her family's debt.

Several minutes later, they reached the house. Dillon and the others met him with enthusiastic greetings. He grinned and briefly answered their questions, but his attention shifted when he spotted Avery leaning against the doorway of the living room. Moving past the others, Aaron approached him.

"A little worse for wear," the man observed with amusement in his voice, "but all in one piece."

Aaron nodded. "I hear I have you to thank for my early release."

Avery shrugged. "When I heard what you did, I couldn't very well just sit by and do nothing."

"How did you do it?"

"Well, here's the thing: when I was younger, I happened to be a rather prolific gambler. I quit at my father's request; however, I was quite good. Turns out I still am."

Aaron raised his brows, but Avery continued.

"Now, before you object to my method, let me assure you that I didn't play against anyone who couldn't afford it. I made certain of that. I knew you wouldn't want anyone else to end up in the workhouse so you could go free."

Aaron gave it a second of thought, and then smiled. Right now, he was just thankful to have his freedom. He wasn't about to argue over the morality of Avery's actions, especially if no one had gotten hurt in the process.

"Thank you," he said, truly grateful.

Avery grinned. "Not a problem. I also made sure Mr. Darwin won't bother you or the Everns again. If he wants business to continue going well for him, he and his men will stay far away from you."

Relief engulfed Aaron. He wouldn't have put it past Darwin to try to squeeze even more out of Aaron and Lacy if he found the opportunity.

Avery pushed away from the doorway and clapped Aaron on the shoulder. "I'll let you get cleaned up and on your way. I know you didn't come here to see me."

Aaron thanked him again and, after excusing himself from the others, made his way up to his room. Once he started to clean up, it turned out he was even grimier than he thought. One glance in the mirror at the way his ribs showed through his skin proved how much weight he had lost thanks to the meager rations of gruel the wardens saw fit to give their prisoners. He scrubbed up as best he could with his basin of water and went to work on his beard. He had to force himself to slow down to shave. He didn't want to end up cutting himself in haste. Given his halfway-emaciated look, he didn't want to add to it with blood.

When he was nearly finished, someone tapped on the door, and Timothy stepped in. His brother paused. He could well imagine how much worse his condition looked to Timothy. Had their places been switched, he probably would have driven Timothy crazy with his concern.

"I just need a little fattening up," Aaron assured him. "Knowing how Mira will dote, I doubt it'll take long."

Now Timothy smiled and nodded. "Well, it's nothing like what she will make, but I laid out some food downstairs when you're ready."

Aaron turned to his bed—a bed that would feel heavenly compared to the hard boards of the bunk he'd been sleeping on—and grabbed the fresh shirt he had pulled out. He tugged it over his head and then put on a clean jerkin. Following Timothy downstairs, they stepped into the kitchen. A plate of rolls, cheese, and cold meat awaited him. His mouth watered, and his stomach growled in anticipation. In his anxiousness to see Lacy, he hadn't realized just how hungry he was. He was used to forcing the sensation to the back of his mind.

Still, he wasn't quite hungry enough to waste any more time here. He grabbed a couple of the rolls, meat, and thick slices of cheese. After taking a bite, he said, "Let's go." He could eat just as well on the way to Ben and Mira's.

This time Timothy didn't stop him. His brother only smiled, and they turned to leave. Outside, Aaron gulped down the rest of his food, temporarily satisfying his hunger cravings.

No longer partially distracted, his focus centered squarely on Lacy. He'd dreamed of seeing her again, every single day. While not much time had actually passed, the mindset he'd had to let himself sink into to keep from going mad, believing he had years of loneliness ahead of him, made it seem as though it was longer. What would it be like to finally see her and know they could move forward with their future?

He drew a long breath. He'd been far less nervous to actually propose to her than he was at this moment. Everything had happened so fast. She had only just placed her faith in Elôm the same day he had proposed and left. Now that she'd had time to contemplate her decision, she could feel it wiser to change her mind or to move forward more slowly. *Elôm, whatever happens, help me to accept it as Your will.*

He looked over at Timothy. "How has Lacy taken the last couple of months?"

"It's been difficult for her, especially right at first, but I've really seen how her relationship with Elôm is progressing. It's been a hard couple of months, but I think it has made her a much stronger person."

Now Aaron's heart swelled in his chest. That, above all, was worth everything to him.

At last, they stepped into the courtyard of Ben and Mira's house. Aaron had to hold himself back from bolting up to the door. Just before they reached it, it swung open. Ben and Mira waited on the other side, their grins bright enough to erase any clinging darkness of the workhouse. They ushered him inside, and Mira engulfed him in her warm embrace and promptly started fussing over him. Aaron smiled and assured her that he was fine, but his attention was divided. He would apologize later, but right now there was only one person he wanted to see. His eyes swept the foyer before his gaze locked on movement in the doorway across from them.

Lacy stepped into view, and their eyes met. The bustle of activity around him muted. Lacy's eyes sparkled with moisture and a gorgeous grin claimed her face. Elôm help him, she was beautiful. He strode across the room, and she flung her arms around his neck with an adorable little squeal of delight. Aaron grinned as he buried his face in her soft hair and hugged her tightly. Her bulging stomach between them made it a little awkward, but he didn't care in the slightest. They were both together now and nothing would part them for so long again if he had anything to say about it.

When they released each other, her cheeks shone damply, but that captivating smile of hers still rested firmly in place as she gazed up at him. A man could happily forget himself in a gaze like that.

"I'm so happy you're back," she said, the slight waver in her voice betraying the depth of her emotion.

"So am I," he murmured.

He could have just stared down at her for hours, but he let his eyes drop and rested his hand on her stomach, which somehow seemed to have doubled in size since the last time he'd seen her. Was there even any more room for the baby?

"I feel like I could burst," Lacy told him, humor in her voice. She squeezed his hand. "But I think he knew he needed to wait for his daddy."

Every fear that she might have changed her mind evaporated with a burst of joy. The only thing that stopped him from giving her a good kiss right then and there was the sudden exuberant commotion of Lacy's sisters as they joined them. Aaron greeted them happily, laughing at Gwen's rapid-fire questions and comments. He didn't even have a chance to address them all.

Instead of trying, his attention shifted to the girls' mother. She smiled warmly as she approached him, looking healthy and strong. Aaron accepted a hug from her as she thanked him again and again for what he had done for them. Aaron only waved off the thanks. He and Lacy might not be married quite yet, but he saw this lovely group of females every bit as much his family as Timothy. He would do anything to keep them safe.

Mira then ushered everyone into the living room and promptly started fussing over Aaron, just as he'd expected. Now that the initial excitement of his arrival was past, he read the concern creeping into Lacy's eyes as she truly took in his appearance. He assured her that he was perfectly fine, and they sat down together. Mira immediately bustled off to get him some more food. Apparently, she was all prepared. Ben named off a whole list of things his wife had spent the morning making. It all sounded so good that Aaron knew he wouldn't be able to resist any of it.

For the rest of the afternoon, they all sat and talked. Everyone had questions for Aaron, though he kept his account of his time in the workhouse brief. No sense in dwelling on it now. Gwen and Hannah were eager to share with him what they were learning from the meetings and about the friends they were making. Lacy didn't say much, but whenever Aaron looked over at her, she wore a soft, contented smile on her face. Though he remained attentive to everyone, what he really wanted now was a few minutes alone with her—a little time to discuss their future.

The opportunity finally came as evening crept in. Mira and Helen left to prepare supper, and Ben and the girls followed after them. Everyone seemed to understand that Aaron and Lacy might want a short time to talk in private.

The room grew quiet, and Aaron shifted to look at Lacy. She met his gaze and held it for a long moment. She seemed so much calmer and more confident since they were last together. Timothy was right—she was stronger. Aaron could sense the ease she felt in her relationship with Elôm. Nothing could have made him happier.

"I missed you," he murmured.

Her lips turned up slightly. "I missed you too. Every single day I prayed that Elôm would bring you back safely."

"And He did."

Her smile grew. "He did."

Aaron gazed at her lips, and the pull to kiss her almost overpowered him, but he waited. Focusing on her eyes again, he asked, "Do you still want to get married?"

Her eyes widened. "Of course," she said with none of the uncertainty of when he'd first asked. "Do you?"

He broke into a smile. No words could describe just how much he did. "Yes. When?"

Lacy rubbed her belly, a contemplative look on her face. "I would like to before the baby comes if possible."

Aaron raised his brows. That didn't give them much time, if any. Not that he would complain.

"Ben and Mira said we could have the wedding here," Lacy continued. Obviously, she had already given this thought. "It doesn't have to be anything more than a simple ceremony. That is all I want."

She looked at him as if hoping he would agree. Aaron smiled and reached up to brush his finger along a loose strand of her rich hair. With her looking at him like that, he would agree to anything. "That is all I want, too."

"ARE YOU NERVOUS?" Timothy asked.

Aaron looked over at him where they waited in Ben and Mira's living room with the other men. "No."

It was true. He couldn't really say he felt any nerves or uncertainty over making the biggest decision of his life—only eagerness. Exactly two months ago, he had walked into the workhouse not expecting to walk back out for at least a couple of years. Now, today, he was going to marry the only woman he had ever loved. He had begun to doubt over the last couple of days if they would make it to this point before the baby arrived, but they had. Any moment, Lacy would walk through the door, and they would become husband and wife. He was tempted to go find her right now.

Forcing himself to remain patient, he looked around the room at their small gathering so far. It would be just Lacy, her family, Ben and Mira, and Alex. After all, without him, this wedding wouldn't be happening. It only seemed right that he be there. He'd seemed surprised yet honored when Aaron had extended the invitation. Despite a rocky start, Aaron was beginning to consider him a good friend. Not just anyone would have gone through the trouble to get the money needed to pay off the debt, especially considering everything he could have done with that money.

Timothy stood beside Aaron as they waited. He would perform the ceremony. While they would need someone like Prince Daniel to eventually make the marriage official by law, all that mattered right now was that they were married before Elôm.

Aaron looked down and straightened his jerkin, but he snapped his head back up as someone entered the room. Mira bustled in, her eyes sparkling with a grin.

"She will be ready in a moment."

Aaron's heart kicked and sped up. His bride was about to arrive. He could barely keep himself still. No doubt the others found it highly entertaining, but they were the last people on his mind. Shortly after Mira came Lacy's sisters, each with a grin to rival Mira's. They took their seats, but Aaron kept his eyes focused on the door.

At last, he caught the muted sound of soft footsteps. A second later, Lacy's mother guided her into the room. Aaron sucked in his breath. Lacy wore a simple blue dress that barely fit around her midsection, but even rags couldn't have diminished her beauty. Her mother and sisters had braided her hair and woven in pale blue flowers from Ben and Mira's garden.

Before he even realized what was happening, moisture blurred her face and burned his eyes. He blinked hard, but it didn't disappear completely, and he had to clear his throat. He thought briefly of the times when he had visited her in the tavern and thanked Elôm those days were in their past.

Today marked the beginning of their future. Lacy had faced so much. All he wanted was to give her the most wonderful life he could from this moment forward.

She seemed to know what he was thinking because her smile bloomed dazzlingly as their eyes met. When she reached him, he took her hands, and her warm fingers squeezed his tightly. He searched her gaze for any signs of uncertainty but found only anticipation. What an honor to know that she had seen the very worst of men and yet trusted him enough to join their lives together. He would work hard every day to prove himself worthy of that trust.

Everything grew quiet around them, and Timothy spoke up, beginning the process of their union. Aaron would have to admit later that he barely heard a word of it. His heart thumped too loudly as he focused on his bride. He never imagined back in Dunlow that he would one day be blessed in such a way.

A few minutes later, Timothy handed Aaron and Lacy each one of the cast bronze rings they'd had made. They were far from perfect, having been made in haste, but even pure gold wouldn't have made them any more precious to Aaron.

Now came their vows. Aaron promised to love and protect this woman every single day for the rest of his life. He slipped the ring onto her finger and stared into her eyes as she said her vows. Her eyes grew a little teary, but the smile he'd fallen in love with never left her face. Then she slid her ring onto his finger.

When at last Timothy pronounced them husband and wife, Aaron drew Lacy close and kissed her until they both needed air. Rosy-cheeked, she grinned up at him, and only then did Aaron notice how everyone clapped and happily cheered them on.

Aaron rested his forehead against Lacy's. "How does it feel to be Mrs. Silvar?"

Still grinning, she answered, "Wonderful." And then she tipped her chin up to kiss him again.

The wedding celebration consisted simply of sitting and talking together through the morning and into the afternoon. There weren't enough guests for a proper party, nor would Lacy have been up to such a thing. But Aaron didn't need a party, or gifts, or anything of the sort. He had his wife, and he had his freedom. That was enough. It meant everything to him just to be able to sit with her snuggled into his side—to wrap his arm around her and hold her close for as long as he desired without it being improper, to gaze at her until she noticed and blushed, to give her soft kisses whenever the inkling arose. However, everyone was probably about ready to start rolling their eyes at him if he did it much more. He was getting down-right anxious for a little time in private with his new bride. Perhaps they could sneak off for a bit before Mira's planned dinner. He had to hold back grinning to himself.

His thoughts now turned to planning their getaway. If they had their own home, he'd just carry her off and forget dinner all together. Mira would have understood. But they didn't even know where they would live yet. In the whirlwind leading up to today, they hadn't discussed it. It was assumed that they would stay here, especially with Lacy so close to having the baby. Beyond that, they would have to figure things out along the way.

He was about to whisper his plan in her ear when she suddenly went rigid in his arm. She gasped and grabbed at her midsection. Aaron sat up straight and shifted to face her.

"What's wrong?"

She sat for a moment, her mouth open partially before looking at him. "The baby. I think it's coming."

Aaron's heart collided with his ribs. "Are you sure?"

Lacy looked across at her mother and then nodded. "Yes."

Aaron's pulse sped up, prompting him to jump into action…but doing what? Uncertainty held him in place. He stared at Lacy, half expecting the baby to be born right there in front of him.

"What do we need to do?" he finally managed.

Helen rose from her chair, calmly taking control of the situation. She spoke and moved as if there was no great urgency, though it did little to calm the pounding in Aaron's chest. His wife was about to have their baby!

"Lacy, why don't you go get changed into something more comfortable. The girls and I will start gathering things."

Ben also rose and spoke with far more confidence in his tone than Aaron possessed at the moment. After all, with five grown children, he was significantly more experienced at this than Aaron was.

"I'll go get the midwife," he said.

As he left the room, everyone started moving around at once, Gwen chattering excitedly. Aaron focused on Lacy as she slid forward in her seat. He stood up quickly and helped her to her feet. They walked together out of the room as the rest of the women bustled off to the kitchen or wherever they were going. At the stairs, Aaron stopped and turned to Lacy.

"I can carry you upstairs."

She gave him a gentle smile. "That's sweet of you, but I can manage right now. My pains aren't bad just yet. My water just broke."

Aaron looked at her. Whatever that meant. Growing up in an all-male household had put him at a severe disadvantage in this situation. He hadn't known his mother long enough to learn things like this. Thankfully, there were more than enough females around now to help out.

She then reached for his arm. "But you can help me up the stairs."

Gladly. Aaron took her hand and wrapped his other arm around her back to support her. They climbed the stairs slowly, Lacy holding her stomach with her free hand. At the top, she led him down to her room. Aaron nudged the door closed when they stepped inside.

Lacy pulled gently out of his grasp and walked across the room. "Let me get a nightgown."

She reached into the wardrobe and pulled out a white slip of fabric that tied up the front. Laying it across the bed, she stopped and faced him. She seemed suddenly shy and a bit uncertain as she peeked up at him through her lashes.

"Will you help me with my dress? I can't reach the laces."

Aaron's heart thumped again. This wasn't how he'd expected their first moments alone as newlyweds would go, but then he'd never imagined becoming a father on the same day he'd become a husband either. Nothing about this was ordinary, yet he thanked Elôm for every bit of it. He stepped closer, and she turned her back to him. Carefully, he loosened the laces of the dress and helped her out of it.

When she caught him staring at her, she ducked her head with a flash of self-consciousness in her expression. "I must look like a whale."

Aaron grinned. That certainly wasn't what he was thinking. "I think you're beautiful." Belly and all, she was the most gorgeous thing he had ever laid eyes on.

Her cheeks turned rosy with an adorable smile, and he gave her a good kiss before helping her slip into her nightgown.

Lacy then sat down on the edge of the bed. A moment later, a wince crossed her face, and she gripped the post of the footboard.

Aaron put his hand on her shoulder, concern rushing in. "Are you all right?"

She closed her eyes and didn't answer for a moment, but then looked up at him. "Yes, but I think the contractions are getting stronger."

Aaron glanced toward the door. "Do you want me to get your mother?"

Lacy rested her hand on his arm now, and her smile returned. "I'm sure she'll be up here shortly, and it's not going to happen that fast, unfortunately. At least, I doubt it."

Aaron let out another heavy breath. He should have been more prepared. As little as he knew about this, he did know it wouldn't be easy for Lacy. If only he could change that. Unsure of what else to do but make sure she knew just how deeply he cared about her, he dropped down to his knee and took her hands in his.

"I just want you to know something. Things might be uncertain around us, but I don't ever want you to worry that I won't always love you or our child. Nothing about the past or future will change that. Today is a fresh start. There will be no looking back."

Moisture gushed into Lacy's eyes. She leaned closer to him and cupped his face with her hands. "Thank you for being so wonderful."

She kissed him then, a long, deep kiss that he gladly returned. When they parted, he whispered, "I love you."

"I love you too."

A moment later, someone tapped on the door. Aaron pushed to his feet, though he kept hold of one of Lacy's hands.

"Come in," she called toward the door.

It opened, and Helen stepped inside, her arms full of fresh, clean towels. Mira and the girls appeared next with more towels, blankets, a basin, and pitchers of water. Seeing it all added a whole new level of reality to the situation.

Aaron stayed with Lacy as the women fussed and prepared the room for the delivery. However, when the midwife arrived, she shooed Aaron out of the room and the door closed behind him. He just stood in the hall for a moment, dealing with the dismissal. He wanted to stay at Lacy's side and see her through this, especially with the pain he had seen creeping into her expression. It would only get worse from here, yet he couldn't be there to support her.

With a sigh, he trudged downstairs and into the living room where he found the men sitting. Ben rose to meet him and gave him an encouraging thump on the back. "This is it; you're going to be a father."

"How long does it usually take?"

"Hours."

Aaron winced. "How many hours?"

Ben offered a sympathetic smile. "With our first child, Mira was in labor for thirteen hours."

Aaron lifted his brows. Thirteen? He sank down into a chair. "And that's...normal? Mira and the baby were fine?"

Ben nodded as he resumed his seat. "Mothers and newborns are heartier than you think. It's all part of the natural process."

Natural or not, this wait would be difficult, especially when he wouldn't be there to make sure Lacy was all right. He blew out a long breath and rubbed the palms of his hands along his pants. He hadn't thought about his mother's death in a long time, but the memories crept in now. She had died giving birth to Timothy. What if he lost Lacy the same way?

He gave his head a stern shake. No. He wouldn't think about that.

"She will be fine."

Aaron looked up at Timothy's voice. His brother's eyes conveyed understanding. Aaron forced a smile. His greatest comfort in all of this was that he knew Timothy would be praying for Lacy and the baby the entire time.

Aaron paced the living room. Five hours. He'd hardly sat still for five hours. Every so often, he heard a faint cry from upstairs, and his gut wrenched. All he wanted was to race up to his wife, but, as Ben had said, this was a natural part of the process. Still, to have his wife in such pain… He rubbed the back of his neck. It just didn't seem right that he couldn't do anything about it. And to think, they could have several hours left to go.

He sat down again, though he rubbed his hands together, unable to stop moving completely. He then bowed his head and prayed another prayer for his wife and child—one of several dozen he had murmured over the last hours. When he raised his head again, he scanned the room. Even Alex had remained. Ben had offered them food from the meal Mira prepared, but Aaron had declined. He wasn't going to eat his wedding dinner without his bride. His stomach was a snarled mess anyway.

In what would surely be a futile attempt to relax, Aaron rested his head back against the chair. Right then, another cry came from upstairs. This one, however was different—a squalling cry of a baby.

Aaron jumped to his feet. "Did you hear that?"

No one said a word as the cry came again, echoing in the house. All at once, the men surrounded him, slapping him on the back and offering congratulations, but all Aaron could really hear was the glorious sound of the newborn's cries. Everything inside him shouted to run to his child and wife. He focused on Ben.

"Should I go up there?"

Surely, the women wouldn't keep him out.

Ben gripped his shoulder, his smile full of understanding.

"Don't worry; they'll come and get you just as soon as they've finished cleaning things up a bit."

Aaron's breath gusted out of his lungs. More waiting? He started to pace again. The last few hours had been torture, but this reached a whole new level. Was Lacy all right? The baby sounded healthy, but what if something was wrong? He couldn't hear it crying anymore. Was that normal? Every minute dragged out. He'd probably crossed the room nearly a hundred times when he finally turned and spotted Hannah in the doorway. He ran to her and grabbed her shoulders.

"Are they all right?"

She grinned at him and nodded. "Yes, they are both fine. Lacy is waiting for you."

Before she even finished, Aaron dashed past her and up the stairs, taking them two at a time. The moment he stepped into the bedroom, his eyes locked on Lacy. Her face was pale and matted hair stuck to the sheen of sweat around her forehead and neck. However, her lips lifted in a smile when she saw him—a tired, yet happy smile that told him she truly was all right. Relief washed straight through him, all the way down to his feet.

That's when his eyes fell on the little bundle wrapped up on her chest.

"Come and meet your son," she said.

That same stinging moisture that had attacked his eyes when Lacy first stepped into the living room as a bride assaulted him again as he walked around the bed to her side. There, peeking out from the soft blue of the blanket were bright pink cheeks, a squashed little nose, and dark lashes. His heart ceased beating, and the moisture almost spilled from his eyes. He'd never in his life seen something so precious.

"He's perfect," he murmured.

He sat down carefully on the edge of the bed, unable to take his eyes off the infant—off his *son*. Nothing really registered around him—not the women who finished cleaning up the room, nor the other men when they were allowed to come in for a brief visit to see the baby. All that claimed his attention now were this perfect child and his lovely wife.

At last, Helen and Mira ushered everyone out. With a final check with Lacy to make sure she was comfortable, they too left the room. The door closed and everything grew quiet except for Lacy's steady breathing and the little smacking sounds coming from the baby's lips. Aaron just stared, mesmerized, for another couple of minutes. Finally, he got up slowly and walked around to the other side of the bed. After pulling off his boots and jerkin, he lifted the covers and crawled carefully in next to Lacy. She grinned at him as he settled in beside her.

"Do you want to hold him?"

The emotions whirling inside him didn't even let him answer, but she must have seen it in his face. Gently, she lifted the baby and shifted enough to lay their son in his arms. As he cradled the baby, he couldn't keep from grinning. He'd never held a baby except for Timothy, and that was so long ago. The infant was so tiny and helpless. Aaron silently vowed right there to do everything in his power to protect his son and raise him to be a good man. He cleared his throat and looked at Lacy, who leaned against his shoulder.

"What do you want to name him?"

She gazed lovingly at their son. "Isaac Josan Silvar." She lifted her eyes to his face. "My father and yours. Do you like it?"

Aaron's smile widened, though his voice came out choked. "Yes." He shifted his attention back to the baby. "Hello, Isaac. You've got two very strong names from two very special men. One day, your mother and I will tell you all about both of them."

Turning to Lacy once more, he tipped his head toward hers to share a soft kiss.

CHARACTERS

Aaron—A half-crete and former miner from Dunlow. Timothy's older brother.

Alex Avery—An old friend of Daniel's who assassinated Emperor Daican.

Banson—Mr. Darwin's debt collector.

Ben—Wealthy merchant and leader of the believers in Valcré.

Darwin—A wealthy businessman in Valcré.

Elôm (EE - lohm)—The one true God of Ilyon.

Gwen—Lacy's youngest sister.

Hannah—Lacy's middle sister.

Helen—Lacy's mother.

Lacy—A barmaid at the Briar Pub in Valcré.

Matthias Artel—A merchant and part of the congregation in Valcré.

Mira (MEER - uh)—Ben's wife.

Tess—An older barmaid at the Briar Pub.

Timothy—A half-crete young man from Dunlow, and the Resistance's spiritual leader. Aaron's younger brother.

Victor—Owner of the Briar Pub.

About the Author

JAYE L. KNIGHT is an award-winning author and shameless tea addict with a passion for Christian fantasy. Armed with an active imagination and love for adventure, Jaye weaves stories of truth, faith, and courage with a message that, even in the deepest darkness, God's love shines as a light to offer hope. When not writing fantasy, she dabbles in contemporary romance under the name Jaye Elliot.

To learn more about Jaye and her work, visit:
www.jayelknight.com

Milton Keynes UK
Ingram Content Group UK Ltd.
UKHW010825230424
441593UK00002B/18